128

SAVING LOVE

BROTHERHOOD PROTECTORS WORLD

JEN TALTY

Twisted Page Press LLC

BROTHERHOOD PROTECTORS

ORIGINAL SERIES BY ELLE JAMES

Brotherhood Protectors Series

Montana SEAL (#1)

Bride Protector SEAL (#2)

Montana D-Force (#3)

Cowboy D-Force (#4)

Montana Ranger (#5)

Montana Dog Soldier (#6)

Montana SEAL Daddy (#7)

Montana Ranger's Wedding Vow (#8)

Montana SEAL Undercover Daddy (#9)

Cape Cod SEAL Rescue (#10)

Montana SEAL Friendly Fire (#11)

Montana SEAL's Mail-Order Bride (#12)

SEAL Justice (#13)

Ranger Creed (#14)

Delta Force Strong (#15)

Montana Rescue (Sleeper SEAL)

Hot SEAL Salty Dog (SEALs in Paradise)

Hot SEAL Hawaiian Nights (SEALs in Paradise)

SAVING LOVE

A Brotherhood Protectors Novella

Book 1 in the Saving Series

Welcome to my brand-new *Saving Series* in the Brotherhood Protectors world. I hope you will enjoy this as much as you did the *Out of the Wild series* in the same world. I want to thank Elle James for this wonderful opportunity!

For Kimberly. Thanks for all that you do!

CHAPTER 1

ALABAMA LOVE MADE the turn into the Broken Spur Ranch with a little too much acceleration of the gas pedal. She'd spent the last three weeks of her life trying to convince herself that she'd made the right decision by changing her plan at the very last minute. However, her near empty bank account reminded her that she had to find work, and fast.

She drove past a shiny SUV and stared at what could only be described as a massive log cabin while big white snowflakes dropped from the sky. Each time she pulled into the small parking area by the garage, she couldn't stop staring at the unique structure. She'd never seen anything like it in her entire life. Well, she'd seen mansions before. Hell, she'd lived in one. But a log cabin that had to be a good five to six thousand square feet?

Never.

Not to mention the real live cowboy that lived inside. If she were any other woman, she'd probably be falling at his feet, like she suspected every female in a hundred-mile radius did. But she'd keep sexy Dakota Newark at a safe distance. No matter how nice he seemed, he'd eventually show his true colors.

They always did.

A large porch wrapped around the front and side of the house, and she loved how it wrapped all the way around to the back. She'd only been inside the house twice. Considering a single father lived there, the décor was impressive with its masculine country feel. It was a unique blend of leather and lace, literally. And he kept the place spotless.

She glanced in the rearview mirror, which showed another mirror facing the car seat. Her son, Wyoming, kicked wildly while he chewed on the corner of his favorite truck. How she lucked out with such a sweet and easy child, considering how he came into this world, would always be a mystery.

She just hoped his father's genetics wouldn't play any role in how Wyoming turned out as a man.

"Ma Ma," Wyoming babbled as he kicked and waved his hands wildly.

"Well, Wyoming. Should I ask him for job recommendations since the waitress job didn't pan out?" Alabama stepped from her vehicle and shivered. Sure, it could be cold in Manhattan, but not this biting cold. She pulled open the back door and lifted her eleven-month-old son into her arms and gave him big kiss on his chubby cheek. He quickly opened his mouth and tried to catch the snow in his mouth. "You're too cute," she said. "I can't believe you're going to be one next month."

Now it was time to put her tail between her legs and ask her landlord for help. He'd offered enough times. He'd even offered his nanny, though Candice hadn't been too keen on the idea without proper compensation and no way would Alabama let Dakota pay his nanny on her behalf. Besides, Alabama didn't like Candice. She'd seen a few behaviors that the nanny had exhibited that made Alabama uncomfortable.

She tossed her purse over her shoulder and took a step toward the tiny house she rented from Dakota. "Can you believe spoiled mama is living in something the size of what used her shoe closet?" It amazed her how quickly she'd become accustomed to having nothing to her name and only a few dollars in her pocket. Of course, it had been an easy decision once her son had come into this world.

Her only concern was making sure Wyoming had everything he needed, which meant she had less than a month to find a job before what little money she had left ran out, and then she was really screwed. The underground had gone above and beyond the call of duty. They had kept her and Wyoming safe and gave them food and shelter much longer than they did most women on the run.

But when Chauncey handed her the keys to this clunker and a chunk of cash, he told her she was on her own. That there was no looking back.

"Do I wait for Candice to leave? Or shall we go talk to Dakota now?" She sucked in a deep breath and let it out slowly. For the first time since she left the prison her husband had kept her in, she felt like she could finally relax. Sure, she assumed she was still on a fugitive list, but she'd actually traveled on an airplane last month, and no one looked at her with any suspicion at all. Not to mention, there was no way in hell Josh would ever consider she'd live on a ranch in the middle of nowhere fucking Montana. First off, she couldn't stand animals or pets. She was terrified of dogs, so being around horses was even worse, and the fact that the cattle ran free still made her race from her front door to her car every morning in fear one might actually charge.

She also used to joke she'd been afraid of fresh air. If she wasn't inhaling smoke and exhaust, then what was the point. Big cities. That's where the old her belonged. Her previous self had servants and lived in mansions and got her hair done once a week. Hell, she wouldn't even spend the night in a regular hotel room. It had to be a suite or the penthouse, or she wouldn't go.

Spoiled and entitled would be two words that the

world would use to describe her, only no one knew what went on behind closed doors. She might have had all the comforts money could buy, but she lived in fear.

But that wasn't her life anymore.

The front door flew open, smashing into the side of the log cabin.

"Don't ever come back; you're not welcome here anymore," Dakota said. In the few weeks she'd known him, he'd never raised his voice.

True colors.

Instinctively, Alabama covered her son's ears. She should turn around and follow the path to the other side of the bushes where the tiny house stood, but she was like a doe in headlights.

"You can't fire me," Candice said, pulling a leather bomber jacket over her shoulders. "My grandfather is going to be so pissed. He'll make you hire me back."

"Your grandfather is going to be happy I stopped the cops from arresting you between the pot smoking and the stealing." He planted his hands on his hips. "I gave you a warning when you started dating Chad, and you ignored me. He's bad news, and he's got you doing things, like drugs, that you've never done before."

"I have a medical marijuana card. I have anxiety and pain. It's perfectly legal for me to have it."

"That's bullshit and you know it." He shook his head. "And you're not allowed to be on it while employed as a childcare provider, and you never told me, but it doesn't matter at this point. Just leave, Candice. And stay away from my girls. Don't make me regret going easy on you."

Candice flipped her long hair and pushed out her hip. "I'm going to tell everyone what a pervert you are. I'll tell Hank Patterson you made a pass at me. That you tried to rape me. Everyone will have to believe me."

"I wouldn't do that if I were you," Dakota said.

"Oh, so now you're threatening me? I need to be recording this," Candice said. "That way I can show everyone what a violent man you are."

Violent?

Could he really be like that? No. He was different. He had to be different.

Alabama really needed to slip away. She shouldn't be listening to this, only all she could think about was how crazy his nanny sounded and the potential job opportunity it created.

Dakota held up his phone. "I already am," he said with a smile. "I thought it might be a good idea considering you've lied about a few things in the last twenty-four hours."

"You asshole," Candice said under her breath. "You have no proof it was me who stole anything. For all you know it could have been your housekeeper. Or maybe it was that bitch over there." Candice pointed to Alabama. "You don't even know anything about her, and she's been living in your backyard. For all you know she's some big con artist sent here to rob you blind."

Wonderful. She pushed out a puff of air, wishing she could slink under a rock. Instead, she just stood there like an idiot.

"Stop blaming others. The pawn shop security camera has you on video pawning my late wife's ring," Dakota said. "Now get off my ranch. Stay away from me and stay away from my girls, or I will make your life a living hell."

"Lunar wouldn't appreciate the way you're—"

"Don't you ever talk about my wife." Dakota took two steps forward and stopped, shaking out his hands. "You barely knew her. Now leave before I change my mind and call the locals."

"Oh, fuck you," Candice said under her breath as she made a beeline for her SUV.

"Uh-oh, Daddy. Candice swore," River said as she skipped through the front door wearing her pink tutu, cowboy boots, and a fleece jacket, unzipped. That little girl beat to the tune of her own drummer, but it was a shocker the poor kid wasn't an icicle. "She should have her mouth washed out with soap. Isn't that what Pappy used to do with you when you swore?"

"He sure did," Dakota said. He held the door open as his big yellow dog raced past, wagging his massive tail. Only about an inch of snow stuck to the grass, but Buster, the crazy dog, managed to stir it all up.

"Oh, no, no, no," Alabama said under her breath as she held her son tight and tried to climb back in her car before the vicious creature attacked.

"Daddy, you know how Alabama feels about the dog." The little girl's voice was barely audible over the roar of the engine as Candice peeled out of the driveway.

"Buster," Dakota yelled. "Get back here."

The dog kept running.

"Alabama, tell him to sit," Dakota said.

"Sit. Sit. Sit," she said, holding her son as tight as she could.

Thankfully, the animal skidded to a stop, moaned, and plopped to the ground at her feet.

"Come, Buster," he called. This time, the dog took his sweet time heading back to the porch.

"You know he's never going to hurt you." Dakota took the steps two at a time and outstretched his arms. "Hey there, big man. Are you walking yet?"

"He's close. Any day now," she said.

He took Wyoming into his arms and tossed him up toward the sky. "You love the snow, don't you?"

Wyoming let out a belly laugh.

"Snow, yes. The cold? We both can live without." She always tried to keep the small talk small, but Dakota had a way of making her feel comfortable, and that frightened her because she didn't want to rely on him.

For anything.

"It's not so bad," Dakota said. "I'm so sorry you had to witness my confrontation with Candice." He handed her back her son. "I probably could have handled firing her better. I really tried to keep my cool. I could have been a little forgiving of the pot, but she stole my wife's rings, and that's just a low blow."

"That's terrible. I'm sorry she did that." Alabama nodded. The word *fired* bounced around in her mind. She'd interviewed for five jobs, and she hadn't gotten a single offer. The rest of the employment opportunities in the area were for office or sales jobs, but she didn't feel qualified to do them.

But childcare? That she was more than qualified for.

Well, minus the dog.

"I probably should have fired her a month ago. I know she'd never harm my kids, or at least I thought she wouldn't, but these last two weeks she's changed. It's that damn new boyfriend of hers, and no one seems to be able to talk any sense into her. I just can't have that around my children."

"I don't blame you." If anyone had tried to tell Alabama that Josh had a mean streak, not only would she not have believed them, but she would have defended Josh to the bitter end. "Unfortunately, she's a grown woman, and everyone can express their concerns, but it's her mistake to make."

"Maybe, but men like Chad are master manipulators, and he's doing a bang-up job of exploiting her weaknesses," Dakota said. "But you know all about that."

"Excuse me? What does that mean?" Her throat went dry. "Why would I know anything about exploiting people?"

"Nothing. I didn't mean it like that. I just figured like every grown lady you've seen at least one asshole in your life." Dakota shrugged as he patted Wyoming on the head. "This kid is too adorable. Does he ever cry?"

She swallowed her fear. Dakota didn't know anything about her past. How could he? They've had maybe ten conversations since she moved in, and they were all superficial and mostly about kids. Though, there was the one awkward single parent chat when he sort of asked her out, and she flat out said dating wasn't in her wheelhouse. He took it well and had been nothing but a gentleman ever since.

"Trust me, he can toss a fit like every other baby out there," she said. For years, she'd let her husband muzzle her voice to the point she didn't know if she even had one anymore. Now that she could stand on her own two feet, she lacked the necessary confidence to ask for what she wanted or needed.

"Do you have family here?" she asked. "Who's going to watch your girls?"

He ran a hand down his face, scratching at the side of his cheek. "I've got a couple of buddies who have wives who stay at home with their kids so they can help out, I guess," he said. "Didn't you have a job interview today?" he asked. "How'd it go?"

"Unfortunately, there were eight women applying for the same job, and two of them used to work at the diner, so I got a *thanks for coming in, we'll keep your resume on file.*"

"That's never fun. I'm sorry," he said.

"Daddy, we're going to be late," River said as she pushed the dog inside the house before running to her father and hugging his leg. She stared up at him with a smile and stars in her eyes.

Dakota pinched the bridge of his nose. "River, honey. I'm going to have to drop you off while I go get your sister."

River drew her little lips into a tight line. "But, Daddy, you promised you'd stay and watch my dance class. You never stay and watch when it's parent observation. You always have to work, and you always spend more time with Sky."

Fired.

A buddy's wife might be able to help out.

All Alabama had to do was step in and save the day. Just open her mouth and make the suggestion. How hard could that be?

Obviously impossible because she stood there like an idiot, saying absolutely nothing.

Dakota bent over and scooped up his daughter, giving her a kiss on the cheek, only she turned her face, sticking her nose in the air.

"I'm sorry, River. If we didn't have to let Candice go, it would be different," he said. "But I can't leave your sister sitting at the school alone, now can I? Or expect the troop leader to stay with her while I'm an hour late?"

"No, I guess not." River rested her head on her father's shoulder. "But this isn't fair."

Wyoming dropped his head, copying River.

"I have an idea." Alabama adjusted Wyoming on her hip and stiffened her spine. "Why don't I go pick up Sky?"

"I would hate to impose on you like that. I'm sure you have lots to do."

She wanted to laugh but figured that would be rude. "I'm sure looking through the want ads can wait an hour." She pulled her cell from her back pocket and handed it to Dakota. "Put the address of the school in my maps app." She ran her fingers across River's pink dress. "I took dance for years when I was a little girl. Observation days are very important."

"Are you sure you don't mind?" he asked.

"Not at all."

"You're a lifesaver," he said, letting out a long

breath. He set his daughter down. "Go get in Daddy's truck. I'll be right there." He kissed River's cheek.

"Yay." As soon as River's feet hit the ground, she took off running.

"I'll have to call the troop leader and give them your information. You'll need to show your ID," he said as he tapped on the screen of her phone. "It's about a twenty-minute drive from here. I'll give you some cash to get some dinner on the way back, okay?"

She wasn't about to argue that since all she had were dry ramen noodles. "What kind of food would you like me to get Sky? Does she have any dietary restrictions? Or is there something you don't want her to have?"

"She'll want you to stop at the Pig Pit. It's a barbecue place. They do a great pulled pork takeout platter. Just get the big family deal and bring it back here since I'll need to feed myself and River too, and of course make sure there's enough for you and Wyoming."

"Your family has some interesting names," she said with a hint of sarcasm.

"I could say the same about you and your son." He winked.

Butterflies formed in her gut. Every conversation she'd had with Dakota ended up with a tinge of flirtation. Not a lot, but enough to remind her that she was indeed a woman.

Something she had been trying to forget.

Which was impossible when standing in his presence.

Devastatingly handsome would be the only way to describe Dakota with his ice-blue eyes and jet-black hair. And who didn't like a little facial hair on a man? It wasn't a lot, more like a thick five o'clock shadow. Just enough to make her want to reach out and run her fingers across his cheek.

But she refrained.

Her days getting involved with men were over. Even the good ones weren't trustworthy. It didn't matter if a man didn't use a fist to get his point across; she'd learned the hard way that there was always an imbalance of power, and that was not something she could be on board with.

Ever.

"I figured if I was named after a state, so should my kid." God, she hoped he didn't bring up Wyoming's father. Even though she'd created a believable story about what happened to his dad, her throat turned dry thinking about having to tell the tale. In all the conversations she'd had Dakota, not once had he questioned her living alone with her baby. She hoped that continued.

"I might get slapped for saying this, but Alabama is a sexy name." He handed back her cell. "I like the way it rolls off my tongue."

Heat rose to her cheeks. She tried to think of

something to say, but all she did was stand there with her mouth hanging open like an idiot.

"I'll bring back dessert," he said.

"That's not necessary."

"I insist," he said. "I best be going. With you stopping to get food, we'll probably be about a half hour behind you. Here's a key to my house. Make yourself at home. There's even a bottle of red wine I opened yesterday on the bar. Help yourself if you'd like." He held her gaze for a long moment. "Maybe we can share a glass when I get back?"

"Okay." Why the hell did she agree to a drink? No. Just no.

"Wonderful. I've been wanting to get to know you better." He inched closer, resting one hand on her hip. "I think you're a special lady." He pressed his lips firmly over hers and in a firm kiss that lasted longer than appropriate for friends, neighbors, or any two people who weren't romantically involved.

And yet, she couldn't pull away.

That was until her son pressed his palm on Dakota's face.

"I think that's my cue to leave." Dakota smiled. "Thank you. I owe you one."

"I might know of a way you can repay me, but we can discuss that tonight," she said.

"I look forward to some adulting tonight."

Oh, Lord. What the hell did she get herself into?

"I'll carry the ice cream, Daddy."

Dakota handed his little girl the bag. "I'm so proud of you. You're an amazing little dancer."

She did a curtsy. "Why thank you, Daddy."

"Make sure you thank Miss Alabama for picking up your sister so I could stay and watch."

"I will." River skipped across the garage and into the house. The last few years had been rough, but River always took things in stride. Even when Lunar was taking her last breath, River was spreading love and joy. She told her mother that she'd take care of Daddy, and she told him that Mommy was going to a place where she'd no longer feel pain and could look down on them and watch over them.

He blinked, keeping the tears from stinging his eyes. It had been two years since his beloved Lunar had died. Most people told him it was time to move on. Everyone tried fixing him up, but a day didn't go by that his heart didn't ache for what he'd lost and what his girls were missing out on, and he just couldn't bring himself to even look at another woman.

Until Alabama pulled into his driveway with a wad of cash and desperation etched into her scared blue eyes.

He'd seen that look before in a woman, and it ate away at his soul.

But there was more to Alabama than the dark secret that lurked in her past. He could see the hint of the woman she once was and the person she strived to be for her son.

"Daddy!" Sky came racing at him from the kitchen. "Look at the patch I got today." She waved something in front of his face as she flung herself into his arms. Thank goodness his girls took after their mother with their petite frames, because when he'd been eight years old, neither one of his parents could have caught him midair.

"What is it?" He gave her a big bear hug and kissed her cheek before resting her on his hip.

"It's a baking patch, and I brought home a cake that I made all by myself. We can eat it with the ice cream. Miss Alabama already has dinner on the table."

"That's awesome." He set Sky down and wandered into the kitchen. The smell of pork and sweet barbecue sauce filled his nostrils. A plan formed in his brain. She needed a job. He needed a nanny. It should be a union made in heaven. That is only if she wanted that kind of employment. Not everyone was cut out to be a caregiver. So far, she'd interviewed for five very different kinds of positions that had nothing to do with children. Maybe she didn't want to be with kids all day. Maybe she needed a break from her own kid. A lot of moms worked, and there was nothing wrong with that.

Lunar worked, though not full time, but she was dedicated to helping the abused break the chains that held them hostage. Lunar would him to help Alabama any way he could.

"Thanks so much for picking up dinner," he said.

"Not a big deal." Alabama carried her son on her hip as she set the table.

"Let me do that," he said, taking the plates from her hands. "Wait. There are only three here. Aren't you joining us?"

"I don't want to intrude on your family time." She batted Wyoming's hand from her face as he tried to grab her ear.

"Well, I insist." He snagged another plate. "And I won't take no for answer. Nor will my girls. You two do want Miss Alabama to stay for supper, right?"

"Yes!" River twirled around, still wearing her dancing dress.

"Will you? Please?" Sky finished putting the napkins and silverware on the table. "I want you to try my cake."

"I don't know," Alabama said, shifting her nervous gaze between her baby and Dakota. "Spending alone family time is so important."

"Do you have pressing plans?" He suspected she didn't. She'd been in town for less than a week, and the only time she left the tiny house had been for job interviews.

"No. Not really."

"Good. Besides, I have something I want to talk to you about, after we eat. Now let me go get the high chair. It's in storage. Along with the playpen. I'll get that out too. You might like that for when you're outside." Before she could even respond, he ducked back into the garage. In the fourth bay, he'd put all the baby stuff he'd finally planned on giving to Goodwill but had yet to call them to come collect it. Maybe he'd let Alabama go through it and see what she wanted before doing that. He found the two items easily and with more excitement than he understood, practically ran back into the house.

"You really didn't have to go to all that trouble," Alabama said as she rocked back and forth, bouncing up and down with her son, who seemed to be slighted agitated by something.

"It was right in the garage." He unfolded the high chair. "Think he might like pulled pork if we grind it up good?"

"He's a garbage plate. He'll eat anything you put in front of him, but let's not give him too much. He's never had pork before, so I have no idea how he's going to react."

"He'll probably make a mess. That's what my girls did the first time we gave it to them." He tested the high chair, making sure it was secure. "Okay, little man. Are you going to let me put you in this contraption?" Outstretching his arms, he wiggled his fingers.

Wyoming screeched with delight as he flung himself forward.

"Sky, get a handful of Cheerios and put them on the tray," he said.

"I'm shocked he's letting you do that. Normally, he'd rather sit on my lap." Alabama folded one arm across her middle and raised one hand to her face. She bit down on one of her fingernails.

"Let's eat while it's hot." Quickly, he snagged two wine glasses and poured some of his favorite vino. He sat at the head of the table and served up the pork to his two girls before passing it on to Alabama. "This really is the best pulled pork you will ever have."

"It smells delicious," she said.

"It was our Mama's favorite, and Daddy likes to get it at least once a week," River said, lifting the pork sandwich to her mouth. A big chunk fell out the back end and landed on her plate. "But Mama didn't buy it at Pig Pit. She made her own, and it was even more delicious."

"I bet it was. Most mama's cooking is," Alabama said. "Except for mine. I feel sorry for Wyoming because I'm about the worst cook ever." She held a fork with a small amount of pork on it in front of her son.

He took a small bite without grabbing the fork or tossing the food on the floor.

Dakota's girls would have had that barbecue sauce on the ceiling by now.

"I can't believe that's true," he said.

"I have a couple of things I can cook well, but what I really need is a cooking class," she said.

"I'm sure a good cookbook will help, and I've got tons in the cabinet next to the fridge. Help yourself."

"Thanks. I appreciate it," she said with a strained smile.

"Miss Alabama. May I ask you something?" Sky set her fork on her plate and wiped her fingers on her napkin.

It was hard not to puff out his chest with pride over the way his daughter behaved. Some moments, it was hit or miss with his girls.

"Of course," Alabama said.

"My mama named me Sky because she gave birth to me outside while she and Daddy were on vacation. I came before the ambulance could get there."

"You came so fast, Daddy barely had time to call 9-1-1," he said with a laugh. "We were torn between Star and Moon."

"That's because our mama's name was Lunar," River said.

"In the end, we decided that the sky holds the stars and moon together over the earth, so we named you Sky." He reached across the table and batted River's nose. "And we decided to name you River because while mama was pregnant with you, we used to go sit in the park by a little creek, and your sister would talk to Mama's tummy, telling you how she was going to take you rafting down the river."

"That's so cute," Alabama said. "But we seemed to have gotten sidetracked, Sky. What was your question for me?"

"I know my dad was given the nickname Dakota because that's where he was born. Why are you and your son named after states?" Sky asked.

"I will gladly answer that when someone tells me what your father's real name is."

He groaned and rolled his eyes. He hadn't been called by his given name since he'd been seventeen, and he didn't want to be called it now.

"He hates that." River covered her mouth and giggled. "It's Wayne."

"The tickle monster is going to come out for that one." He waggled his finger in his daughter's direction before turning his attention to Alabama. "It's your turn."

"For the record, Wayne is a good name," Alabama said. "The story behind my name comes from where my father proposed to my mom, in Birmingham, Alabama. I'm just glad they didn't name me Birmingham." She ran a hand over the bald head of her son. "I named this little guy Wyoming because when he was born, I had planned on moving there, but I ended up in Montana instead."

"While we love the great state of Montana, I think Wyoming is a much better name for a young man."

Dakota stuffed the last bite of his dinner in his mouth before shoving his plate to the side. "Girls, are you all done?"

They both nodded.

"Then why don't you go watch a show for a bit and let me talk to Miss Alabama. We'll let our meal settle and then have some ice cream and cake."

"Okay, Daddy." Sky pushed back her chair and took her sister by the hand. "Wonder what grown-up stuff they have to discuss," she whispered.

"Maybe they're going to kiss," River said, glancing over her shoulder.

Dakota smacked his forehead. "Sorry about that."

"No worries." Alabama lifted her glass and took a small sip. "You have great kids."

"They are pretentious as hell, and when they turn into teenagers, it will most likely be the death of me." He grabbed the bottle and topped off their wine.

"That's usually the way things work," she said.

"Mind if I ask you a really personal question? About Wyoming's father?"

Her eyes grew, and if he wasn't mistaken, she held her breath for a good half a minute before letting it out slowly. She tucked her hair behind her ears. "He's not in the picture."

"I don't mean to pry, but I have a proposition for you that would be mutually beneficial, and I just want to know what the situation is."

"Wyoming's father has made it quite clear that he

doesn't want to be a father. His name is not on Wyoming's birth certificate. He's not a bad person, just not father material, or husband material for that matter." She handed her son a piece of bread. "So, what might this mutually beneficial proposition be?"

"You need employment, and I need a nanny. It's not the best paying job, but it's more than you'd make waiting tables at the diner, and you wouldn't need to hire your own babysitter. I figure I would take your rent off the top of your salary. I can pay weekly, bi-weekly, or monthly. Whichever you prefer."

"Wow. That's quite a generous offer." The corners of her mouth tipped into a smile.

He chuckled. "Looks like you've been thinking about the possibility."

"I'd be lying if I said the thought didn't cross my mind when you fired Candice. I just wasn't sure how to approach you on the subject. I mean, we barely know each other, and I have no qualifications in childcare."

"You're a mother. I'd say that's about the best qualification I could ask for." Of course, he knew that wasn't really true. He'd seen his fair share of bad parenting from both mothers and fathers. But Dakota trusted his instincts, and he believed inherently that Alabama was a good person. Whatever she was running from, it wasn't because she'd done anything wrong.

Quite the opposite.

He could tell.

"There is one big problem with my job," he said. "Sometimes I'm gone overnight, or even for a week. It almost never happens. My boss tries not to assign me a case that's going to take me away from my girls for any length of time, but it could happen. You'd move in here, of course, if I were to be gone overnight. And you'd be paid more, obviously."

"What about the dog? I'm sorry, dogs frighten me, but I hate that he's currently barricaded in the other room. I mean, he's a sweet dog."

Buster. He was going to have to get them used to each other, and quick.

"I can bring him to work with me on some days, but he's a good dog; he listens to the girls, and he listens to you. I know he's got a deep bark. And he makes a lot of noise when people come around, but the only thing he's good for is licking people to death."

"Well, I need the money, and you need a babysitter, so I guess I need to learn to like dogs." She stretched out her hand. "Shall we shake on it?"

"Absolutely." His cell rang. He glanced at the screen. "I'm sorry. That's my boss. I have to take it."

"No worries. I'll start cleaning up from dinner."

"You don't have to do that," he said.

"I don't mind. Besides, that cake really smells good, so the faster this is cleaned up, the sooner I get a piece."

"Then, by all means, have at it." He stood and stepped out into the cold winter night. He leaned against the railing and stared at the Crazy Mountain range in the distance. White clouds floated across the darkening sky. He'd never mind the cold. Having been born and raised in North Dakota, harsh—brutal —winters were the norm.

He glanced over his shoulder. Alabama moved about his kitchen with ease.

"Hey, Hank." Dakota held his cell to his ear. "I'm sure you heard what happened with Candice by now." He scratched at the side of his face. Growing a slight beard had been the one thing he allowed himself that his late wife would have given him hell for. She didn't hate facial hair; she just preferred he didn't sport it.

"I can't believe she stole from you. It's not like her to do something like that."

"Yeah. That was a shocker, but what she stole really broke my heart."

"I'm glad you got the rings back. Did you have the batch of weed you confiscated sent to our friends at the local office?" Hank asked.

"They said they should be able to tell me if it's from a legal farm or if she bought it off the streets, which I'm guessing she did." Dakota pinched the bridge of his nose. "Candice was a great sitter until about three weeks ago, and then weird shit started happening, and I have to think it has to do with that new boyfriend of hers."

"Chad Hooker and he's a smooth-talking, low-level loser," Hank said. "But he has a way with the women and is a master at talking his way out of trouble. Not to mention his family is rich, corrupt, and trying to connect with the big-time mafia, though that doesn't seem to be going their way."

"I felt bad firing her. I respect old man Benny, but I have to protect my girls, and I can't have that shit hanging around my home." Dakota glanced over his shoulder. Alabama loaded the dishwasher while River and Sky sat on the floor with Wyoming playing with a bouncy ball.

"I would have done exactly the same thing," Hank said. "I know that leaves you without daycare. I just assigned Taz a case where he's going to need some tech backup. You can do that working from home."

"I already solved my nanny problem." Two years ago, he left the military to return home to help his wife battle breast cancer. Last year, she lost that battle. Since then, he'd gone through two nannies. Sure, some of his buddies at work were more than willing to help out, but he wanted stability for his girls. He wanted something akin to normal. He wanted permanence for his daughters.

"Oh really, who?"

"Alabama Love."

Silence on the other end of the line.

"Do you think I'm crazy?" Dakota asked as he

stared at the moon dance over the mountaintops. A lone wolf howled in the night.

"No. But we both know she's running from something or someone."

"Yeah, but she's doing it to protect herself and her son," Dakota said. "I've talked to Clayton and Sage about it, and they both agree. We've all seen it before. The question is how well did she cover up her past life and is the man she's running from a powerful one with the means to find her?"

"That is if she didn't kill him," Hank said. "Because we both know that's a possibility too."

Dakota's heart dropped like a cement brick to his gut.

"Do you want me to dig into her past?" Hank asked.

"If we do that, we run the risk of poking a hornet's nest that could land right on my front doorstep."

"If we don't, you run the same risk, and you won't even see it coming. Take the time to do it and use company resources. Fly as low as you can under the radar but do it."

"Lunar would just tell me to make sure Alabama and her son had a safe environment where they didn't have to constantly look over their shoulders wondering when the next fist was going to land in their faces." His wife had a huge bleeding heart, especially when it came to battered women and children.

She dedicated her life to helping them find safe havens.

He could be that place for Alabama and Wyoming.

"She would also want you to make sure her girls were safe, and that's what you're doing," Hank said. "I'm going to take you out of the rotation right now and use you in-house, at least until we know more about Alabama. You won't be able to give any case I hand over your full attention until you know more."

"You're right. Thanks. I'll be in the office first thing." Dakota ended the call.

CHAPTER 2

Dakota always preferred the great outdoors to sitting behind a computer, but sometimes his job required massive amounts of research and piles of paperwork.

Though, right now, his so-called research was for personal reasons. He wished he didn't have to take advantage of his position and his experience in the military, but he had to keep his family safe.

As well as Alabama and her young son.

"Where did she say she was from?" Kujo asked as he strolled across the main room at the Brotherhood Protectors office.

A few years back, as the Brotherhood grew, Hank built office space and staffed it with a couple of full-time techies and support personal. When not on assignment, any of the protectors could come in and use the offices and state of the art equipment for their cases or to offer assistance to those out in the field. It also allowed all the members to get to know the new recruits and develop the necessary trust they needed when working on dangerous missions together.

"A small town in upstate New York called Clifton Park." Dakota shuffled some papers around on the desk he'd chosen to work from. There were eight in the main room along with four other private offices, but those were generally used for phone calls or the occasional private conversation. But mostly all the protectors preferred working in groups.

A collective think tank of sorts.

"So, she's probably really from the other side of the country," Kujo said. "Or, close to that small town, keeping her lie close to the cuff."

"And then there is her name. Alabama." Dakota knew there was a story behind every fake name, as with real ones. Usually, it had some meaning. In this case, it could be tied to her family name. "She said she was named after where her father proposed, which was actually Birmingham."

"That's interesting," Kujo said. "We can run her image through records and see if we get a hit."

Dakota nodded as he scratched at the side of his face. He still hadn't gotten used to the light beard. "She mentioned she thought she'd be moving to Wyoming, not Montana."

"Depending on what underground network she

originated from and how long she's been hiding out, she could have picked her location." Kujo slipped behind one of the desks and started tapping at the keyboard in front of him. "And if anyone thought whoever she's running from was onto her location or plans, they would have told her to switch it up." Kujo wasn't telling Dakota anything he didn't already know, but sometimes it was good to speak out loud both the knowns and the unknowns.

"Kind of a brilliant plan to stick her in the middle of the Brotherhood Protectors," Dakota said. "Of course, if she was with the underground, when she surfaced with her new identity, where she went and what she did was up to her, so it's possible they don't even know where she is."

"I struggle with it being a coincidence that she ended up here, and this isn't the Witness Protection Program. Someone on our team would have a hint if that were the case, so either she just tossed a dart on a map, or she knew about the Brotherhood and made her way here," Kujo said.

"But we both have to admit, this is a great place to hide, and Clayton, Sage, and I all know people in the underground."

"That's true. But I would think if she was sent here for protection, someone would have called us." Kujo flipped the computer around. "Trish is running a facial recognition software across social media sites starting in Alabama and New York. We're not hitting any police or government databases, but she'll expand as needed."

"Good. I don't want to flag anything and bring some abusive asshole back into her life, and mine." Dakota also had her fingerprints, but he wasn't going to run them, not yet anyway. Maybe never. She and her son deserved a fresh start.

"I'm only playing the devil's advocate here." Kujo held up his hand as if in protest. "But not every woman who is on the run with a kid is hiding from a douche bag. She could have just kidnapped her kid because the ex-husband got remarried and she didn't want to share."

"Is that what you think?" Dakota had run a million and one different scenarios racing through his mind between last night and this morning. He'd gotten maybe three hours of sleep while he contemplated them all, mulling them over in the ways he thought his late wife might have done. Only, her approach would have been to take care of Alabama and make sure she had a safe environment. Well, Dakota was doing exactly that.

But he needed to know exactly who and what he was dealing with.

And what danger might be lurking around the corner. If he didn't know who the enemy was, he had no way of protecting his family from the threat.

"I have no thoughts or opinions on the matter, currently. She could also just be an uneducated woman with little money searching for a better a life for her and her kid," Kujo said. "But I'd like to see that birth certificate and have a better look at who she is."

"Spend five minutes with her, and you'll know without a doubt she's had an extensive education, but I'm not sure it's a useful one, as in I have this weird feeling she's from mad stupid money." Dakota pinched the bridge of his nose and inhaled sharply. The idea of searching Alabama's things put knots in his stomach. His job often required him to invade people's privacy, but that felt very different, especially when he knew someone was in danger.

He didn't know anything for sure.

But he knew he needed to, for the sake of his girls.

"Why would you say that?" Kujo asked.

"Just the words she chooses to use sometimes. The way she carries herself during a conversation. Lunar came from the kind of wealth that could solve a third world country's problems but chose not to. That's why my late wife went into the kind of work she did and why she stopped speaking to her family a few years after we married. I know that kind of money, and I know someone who is trying desperately to separate themselves from it, but it goes deeper than that, I believe, for Alabama. I think she's accepted being poor as a means of protecting her son, but she hasn't come to terms with the past, not completely."

"You've made a lot of assumptions for someone who has only spent a month with her," Kujo said.

"My wife worked with abused women, and when I wasn't deployed, I volunteered with her. I've seen it a hundred times, and Alabama has that same terrified, yet determined expression etched in her gaze. It's so classic it's almost cliché."

"That might be true, but keep your eyes and ears open. You don't have any of the facts."

"And that's what we're doing here," Dakota said.

"So, what's the plan outside of a slow paper chase?" Kujo asked.

"Tomorrow, while Sky is at a birthday party, she's taking River and her son to that party zone place in town. That will give me and Clayton at least two hours to go through the tiny house."

"I can search her car while she's there," Kujo said.

Dakota leaned back in his chair and swirled it back and forth. "I sent an email to a guy Lunar and I used to know. He ran the safe house for battered women, and I know Lunar helped him make at least two women disappear, but what always bothered me about the way they did things was once the women went underground, Lunar had no idea where they went or if they remained safe. It's got to be ten times harder when kids are involved."

"The bigger problem is that when adults go missing, it's not necessarily a big deal. Adults are allowed to do so if they want. But go missing with kids, and it's criminal."

Dakota didn't like the sound of that. "What if she went missing before she gave birth? Before the father even knew he was going to be a father?"

"Totally gray area," Kujo said with a wave of his hand. "What's the new nanny doing right now?"

"She's just hanging at the house with the kids. They have this entire week off from school."

"Ah. February break."

Dakota nodded. "They go back on Monday, and then her hours will change drastically, but I'm going to let my cleaning service go. They don't do that great of a job anyway, and if Alabama wants the work, it's hers."

"You're getting yourself quite entangled with this young woman," Kujo said. "Are you sure that's what you want?"

"As long as it's the kind of work she wants, and I can provide and pay for it, then absolutely." Dakota knew he was taking a risk, but if he did nothing, or sent Alabama packing, the consequences could be worse.

ALABAMA STOOD in front of the stove and tapped her fingers on the counter as if that would guarantee her lasagna would come out not only looking like perfection, but more importantly, tasting like something other than garbage. She also worried about it boiling over the top of the pan. The one time she tried to make a cake for her husband right before they got married, she made a mess inside the oven.

That had been the first time he used his fists.

It should have been the last.

Buster barked and she jerked.

"Shit," she mumbled as she glanced over her shoulder. Getting used to being around that massive beast wasn't going to be easy. Nor would spending any amount of time with Dakota. The second she'd laid eyes on him, he'd stirred that same raw passion that her Josh had. The kind of desire that started at her toes and burned a path to her lips. She'd fallen so hard and fast for Josh that she never really got to see the real him until it was too late.

Well, that was never going to happen again. A lot of women raised their children alone. She didn't need a man in her life ever again. She could do this on her own.

She bent over and flicked on the oven light as if that would make the timer go any faster. She had no intention of staying for dinner, even though Dakota had insisted when he walked through the door thirty minutes earlier than he said he'd be home. She figured he did that on purpose, which she could understand. He wanted to see how the new girl was handling three kids. Well, the girls she could cope with.

Noodles and meat sauce, not so much.

Thank God she'd already put the food in the oven and was just about done cleaning the kitchen. If he'd seen the mess she'd made, he might have fired her on the spot.

She chuckled. Growing up, her family had maids that came every day and also had a full-time cook. A sweet older woman named Janel who came every day around three in the afternoon to cook the family dinner. When she'd gone off to college, she'd been forced to live in the dorms the first year, but that didn't stop her from hiring a gourmet cook to bring her food every day and hiring someone to clean her room.

When her parents died, things really changed for her. Not so much financially, but her world crumbled. She was lost and didn't know where to turn.

In walked Josh and all the answers.

And when she'd married Josh only ten days after graduation, she'd already hired a full staff which included a couple of cooks and a cleaning lady. She might suck at cooking, but she sure as hell knew how to manage the staff that she now realized she never needed in the first place.

Only, she had no idea if this was going to taste like sewage, or food, but she suspected mac and cheese from a box wasn't exactly what Dakota expected when he added meal preparation to her list of duties.

"Your son is going to be walking any second now." He rested his hands on her shoulders and squeezed.

She jumped, lunging forward, away from his grasp, and knocking over the glass of wine she'd just poured. It tumbled to the wood floor and shattered into a million pieces. "I'm so sorry," she mumbled. Her hands trembled as she knelt, reaching for one of the larger pieces of broken glass.

You stupid bitch.

Why do you make me do this to you?

Josh's voice boomed between her ears. Deep down, she knew Josh wasn't here, and he couldn't hurt her, but spilling wine and breaking an expensive glass, that was exactly the kind of thing that would push him over the edge.

"Don't touch that," Dakota said with a stern voice.

With a shaky finger, she tucked a hair behind her ear. She blinked, fighting back the tears as she stared up at Dakota's intense gaze.

But she didn't see rage glaring from his soft-brown eyes. She saw something that could only be described as concern.

He stretched out both arms and lifted her off the floor.

She wanted to protest, but fear gripped her vocal cords, preventing her from speaking out. If she ever spoke against Josh, he'd more than likely hit her, or at the very least, belittle her.

Pull it together. He's not Josh. You're not in Manhattan. You're safe.

"You're not wearing any shoes, and I didn't want you to cut yourself," he said. "Let me pour you another glass, and I'll clean that up."

"Thank you." She took in a deep breath through her nose and let it out through her mouth. "I hope that wasn't a very expensive or sentimental wine glass."

"We probably bought them at Wal-Mart," he said with a chuckle. "My wife didn't like to spend money on designer things, so we always went with cheap, except for furniture. But even then, she didn't want name brands, just quality."

"Smart woman." Alabama's heart beat so fast she thought she might be having an actual heart attack instead of a panic attack. She continued to control her breathing, quietly, hoping he didn't notice. When she'd first left Josh, she suffered from severe anxiety, something she'd never had before. She'd always been confident. Cocky, actually.

But Josh destroyed her self-esteem.

And stole her life.

"Most intelligent person I've ever known." Dakota swept up the broken glass, wiped up the liquid, and poured them both fresh wine before sitting at the table.

"The girls told me she passed away. I'm so sorry for your loss," she said. Her pulse still pounded frantically in her ears. She shouldn't pry about his personal life, but curiosity got the better of her, and she found herself wanting to know more about the kind of man who seemed to be too good to be true.

"Thank you."

"You've done an amazing job with your daughters. They appear to be handling their mother's passing with a lot of maturity for their ages." Alabama had enjoyed listening to River and Sky talk about their mother with love and admiration. Even though their sadness of her death still rose to the surface, their deep devotion to keeping their mother's memory alive in their hearts shined through.

"Sometimes I think they managed to handle it all better than I have," he said with thick emotion hanging on his words.

"I'm sure it's been difficult for you to do this alone."

"It's been a rough few years, but I promised Lunar and myself that I would give our girls the best possible life I could, and that meant I had to learn to live my life as a single dad. Sucks on some days, but those two little girls are my world, and I would do anything for them."

She clutched at her pendant dangling around her neck. It carried a picture of her and her son on the day of his birth. But behind that was an image of her parents and her when she'd been five years old. It was the only thing she'd kept from her past. The only thing she had linking her to her old life. She missed her parents. She wondered if they hadn't died her junior year in college if she would have fallen so hard and fast for Josh. Maybe they would have seen what a heartless bastard he was and saved her from five years of hell.

"I don't mean to pry, but the girls didn't mention what your wife died from?"

"Breast cancer." He scratched at the side of his face and let out a puff of air. "She was diagnosed when River was two and died two years later. River only remembers her being sick, which breaks my heart. I try to give them all the good memories of their mother as often as I can, but they are my memories, not theirs."

"But they had a loving mother, and they have pictures and videos." Her son, thankfully, would have nothing to remember his father by. "And they have you. They think you walk on water."

"They also think all dads should have wives and have made it their life mission to find me a good one," he said with slight chuckle.

"I'm aware. They showed me a list they have compiled of potential women for you, but they told me they haven't vetted them all yet."

"Vetted? They actually used that word?"

"Oh yeah. Sky even said your boss, Hank, was going to help her with the process."

"Oh, good Lord." He tossed his head back and laughed. "And dare I ask why they showed you this list?"

"They started by crossing Candice off the list."

"Oh, thank God. Besides her basically being a child, she's so not my type," he said.

"She's only five years younger than me."

He arched a brow and glanced to the ceiling. "That makes you twenty-eight?"

"I'll be twenty-nine on Valentine's Day," she said, wishing she hadn't enlightened him on the date of her birthday, much less her age, though now she wondered his and hoped maybe she was under what he considered too young. Sadly, she'd always preferred older men. That's one of the reasons she fell so quickly for Josh.

"I'll have to remember that and treat you to something special." He winked.

She waved her hand. "Oh, no. Please don't. I hate birthdays. And this one is just one shy of a big one."

"You've got to be kidding me. I just turned forty, so you don't get to say that to me. Besides, knowing my girls, they put you on the dating list, so even if they don't know that Valentine's Day is your birthday, they will be up to playing cupid."

"Wonderful," she mumbled. "No offense to your daughters, or you, but I'm not looking."

"Neither am I, but Sky and River have it in their heads that I need a girlfriend. I've explained that I don't. However, they have my stubborn streak and their mother's inability to let things go. I will have a little chat with them, but can we humor them for your birthday? We kind of make a big deal about birthdays because that's a celebration of life and having lost their mother, well, we like to make the living feel important."

How the hell could she say no to that? "As long as it's nothing too fancy, got it?"

"Got it," he said.

The oven dinged.

"Of course, you might fire me after this meal."

His laughter was cut short the second he opened the oven.

She stood and peered over his shoulder. "Oh no. How did that happen?" She stared at the goop that had bubbled over the rim of the metal pan she'd put all the noodles, meat, sauce, and a couple different kinds of cheese in. She'd followed the directions, for the most part, so she wasn't sure why half her concoction was burnt on the bottom of the oven.

He snagged some hot mitts and pulled out the so-called lasagna, setting it on the rack next to the stove. "You overfilled the pan and might have put in too much sauce and cheese, but it smells good." He took a fork and a cut out a small portion. Holding it up to his mouth, he puckered his lips and blew.

For the last few months she'd lived on takeout and the occasional microwavable meal. Back in the day, her palate couldn't tolerate such things, but today, all she cared about was putting calories in her body. Her stomach knotted as she gnawed at her fingernail.

"You look absolutely terrified," he said with an amused smile.

Fear crept up from her toes all the way to the tip of her tongue. If this were Josh standing in front of her, she'd already be on the floor with a few bruises for ruining the oven.

"It would be such a waste if that meal isn't eatable. And I'm so sorry about the oven. I will clean it tomorrow."

He leaned in and kissed her cheek. "Once it cools, I'll scrape what I can, and then it will self-clean. You don't need to worry about it at all." He gave the pasta one more good blow before he shoved it between his teeth. His eyes grew wide before he turned and spit the contents of his mouth into the sink.

She covered her mouth with a gasp, taking two steps back. Her hands trembled. She resented how quickly certain situations would send her spiraling into the scared woman Josh created. When she left, she promised herself she'd never let another man make her feel the way Josh had.

"I can honestly say I've eaten worse."

Panic took over her mind. No matter what she

told herself about how kind Dakota had been since she'd moved in, he was still a man, and he still had fists.

He glanced over his shoulder as he tossed a napkin in the trash. "I'm sorry. I didn't mean to insult you, but you did say it could be bad."

She nodded, trying desperately to control her breathing. She'd never had a panic attack until after she'd gotten married. And in the last couple of years, they came regularly. While in the underground, she developed strategies on how to deal with them, but currently nothing was working. As he closed the gap between them, her lungs burned while she tried to take in a deep breath.

"I'm not going to hurt you." He held his hands up.

Clutching her necklace, she pushed her back against the wall. "I know," she whispered. But she didn't know anything except she felt as though she were still a caged animal.

"You're safe with me," he whispered. "It's just a dinner that didn't come out right and a mess that can be cleaned up. Nothing to get upset over."

Intellectually, she knew that.

But her past reality dictated something entirely different. She opened her mouth but all that came out was some high-pitched strange noise that made her sound like some pathetic person. She cleared her throat. "I'm sorry. I'm just tired. It's been a long day," she managed to croak out in what she hoped was a strong tone.

He reached out and tucked a piece of her hair behind her ear. "You still need to eat dinner. I'm going to order pizza, wings, and salad. Does that work for you?"

"You don't have to feed me. I've got some—"

"I insist." He rested his hands on her shoulders. "I don't know what happened to you, and I'm not going to ask you a lot of questions about it right now, but I want you to know that I will make sure you and Wyoming are always safe in my home."

A burst of rage moved through her bloodstream. "You keep saying that, and I don't understand why. I don't need your protection."

"I've seen this kind of thing—"

"I'm not a client of yours. I haven't hired you to protect me from anything."

"I understand that," he said with an arched brow. "But I've seen women on the run before and—"

"On the run? That's what you think? Wow." She sucked in a deep breath, hoping it would give her some courage as she patted his chest and maneuvered around him. "I suppose your job puts those kinds of ideas in your head. Now, it's getting late, and I need to put Wyoming down. Sorry my dinner didn't work out. I'll do better next time. See you tomorrow morning."

CHAPTER 3

ALABAMA KNEW she'd locked her car. It had been a habit she'd gotten into when she'd first learned how to drive. Never in her life had she forgotten, and she certainly wouldn't have started now.

"I can help buckle him," River said as she slid across the back seat.

"Make sure it goes through the loops on the car seat." Alabama watched while River snapped the belt in place before slamming the door shut. She hugged herself and glanced around and shivered. Not too many people milled about the street. The sun beat down on the snow that had fallen the night before, warming her face, even though the temperatures had fallen below freezing.

Paranoia had become a way of life. She wished she didn't resent it because a healthy dose of fear helped her be super aware of her surroundings.

Which is why she knew the car parked across the street was the same white pickup truck that had been at the party zone forty minutes ago. Could it be possible that the same person also had to go grocery shopping?

Possible in a small town.

But not probable.

She turned and ran right into Candice. "Oh, sorry."

"You should be," Candice said. "And about more than practically knocking me over." She gave Alabama the once-over.

"Like I said, I'm sorry. I didn't see you."

"You should be more careful. The sidewalk can be slippery when it snows. I wouldn't want you to fall down and break a leg."

Alabama swallowed her gasp. That sounded like a threat if she'd ever heard one. "I appreciate the warning."

"I see you have River with you."

"I'm sorry. I really need to go." Alabama didn't have the time, nor the inclination to shoot the shit with Candice. She didn't like her the first time she met her when she'd moved into the tiny house, and she didn't like her now.

"I take it Sky's at Gina's birthday party?" Candice asked with sweetness to her voice, but it came off more as sarcasm than anything else.

"I don't mean to be rude, but—"

"But what?" Candice asked with a smirk. "You stole my job; the least you could do is give me the time of day when I talk to you and ask about the family I cared for."

Alabama stuck her index finger in her ear and wiggled. "I did nothing of the sort."

"Right. I bet you stole his dead wife's rings and dressed up to look like me when you tried to pawn them off."

"That's the most obscured thing I've ever heard. I don't have time for this," Alabama said as she took a step to the right. Before she'd met Josh, she could handle confrontation. She didn't like it, but she knew how to deal with it appropriately.

After Josh, she wanted to avoid it all costs, and she still felt that way and especially with someone like Candice. She could really bring the kind of attention to Alabama's life that she didn't need.

Candice blocked her. "I needed that job, and you put ideas in Dakota's head."

"I had nothing to do with you getting fired. Now if you will excuse me, I need to go." The hair on the back of Alabama's neck stood at attention. Between Candice confronting her with the kids in the car, and some random person sitting in a white truck staring at her, she wanted to crawl right out of her skin. Was this how the rest of her life was going to be? Would she ever feel safe again?

"You had everything to do with it. Ever since you

showed up, Dakota started finding fault in everything I did, and I would wager that you were the one putting those thoughts in his ear."

"You're nuts. Now leave me alone."

"You are going to regret crossing me." Candice took off across the street and disappeared down the alley behind the coffee shop.

Alabama took a few minutes to calm herself down before scurrying across the hood of her vehicle. She climbed in behind the steering wheel and let out an exasperated sigh.

"What did she want?" River asked.

"Nothing really."

"Daddy said if she tried to contact us, we were to tell him. Should I be telling him this?"

Alabama glanced in the rearview mirror and smiled. "If that's what your father wants, we should absolutely tell him we ran into Candice. She's just upset she's no longer your nanny."

"Well, she shouldn't have taken my mama's wedding rings and then tried to sell them. Daddy doesn't cry, but he cried when he thought those were gone for good." River swiped at her cheeks. "I don't like it when Daddy cries."

Alabama turned and reached over the seat, taking River's hand in hers. "Crying isn't always a bad thing, even when it's because we're sad. Sometimes our bodies just need to cry so we can feel better. Your dad loved your mom. He still does. That's a good thing. A very good thing. Hold on to that. Not everyone has something as special as what your parents had."

"You know what?" River asked. "I'm glad Candice got fired. She wasn't very fun. She always complained about having to do things with us. You're so much better, and I bet my mama would have liked you."

"I bet I would have liked her too." Alabama gave River's hand a good squeeze. It would take fifteen minutes to drive to the party to get Sky, which was ending in about ten minutes. "We better get going," Alabama said, hoping that stupid white truck stayed put, only it was gone when she pulled out into the street.

Unfortunately, she spied the pickup when she turned onto the main drag.

Shit.

Who the hell was following her?

And why?

Maybe it was Candice. It could be. Made sense. But who was with her?

Or maybe Dakota stuck one of his co-workers on her, but something told her if that were the case, she'd never know she was being followed.

Which could only mean one thing: Josh found her.

Tears stung the corners of her eyes. No way. He couldn't have. She'd been so careful and done every-thing the underground had told her to do. She even went to a different state than what she originally had planned and didn't tell a single soul.

Except Chauncey, who told her to head this way.

She should be safe, unless Chauncey was a bad guy and knew who she was.

When she pulled up to the house where Sky was, the white truck turned down another street and disappeared. Alabama didn't know if that was good or bad. "Let's go get your sister," she said.

"We can stay in the car. I'll take care of Wyoming," River said.

"I don't like leaving him in the car, ever. It's not a big deal." She stuck her head inside the back seat when she saw the pickup drive past. She tried to get a good look at the driver, but the windows were tinted. Her heart hammered against her chest. For a split second, she thought about calling Dakota, but what would she say?

"River, have you ever seen that white pickup truck before?" She put Wyoming on her hip and took River by the hand before heading up the walkway toward the house.

"Yeah. That's Chad. Miss Candice's friend. Daddy really doesn't like him."

Alabama let out a sigh of relief. While she didn't like that Candice and her boyfriend were following her, it was a hell of a lot better than her husband who, she knew without a doubt, would kill her with the snap of his fingers. "We'll be sure to tell your father about him too." She tapped at the front door, glancing over her shoulder. Candice and the white truck seemed to be gone, but Alabama's nerves crept back into her gut, swirling around like a tornado.

Having attention drawn to herself by having a conflict with someone in town wouldn't be a good idea.

"Oh. Hello. You must be Alabama. I'm Teresa. It's nice to meet you. Sky has been talking you up all day." Teresa pulled back the front door and stepped aside. "Isn't this little boy adorable."

Wyoming decided to act all shy and bury his head on Alabama's shoulder. He wrapped his thick fingers around her neck. "He didn't have a long enough nap today," she said.

"And how are you doing, River?" Teresa asked.

"Good." She hugged Alabama's leg.

Teresa patted River on the head. "Why don't you wait right here, and I'll go get Sky."

"Thanks," Alabama said.

As soon as Teresa disappeared into the other room, River tugged at Alabama's coat.

"She has a crush on Daddy, but Daddy says she's way too high-maintenance," River said. "I don't know what that means, but she's never been on our list. She treats me like I'm a baby, and she's always showing up at the house with weird healthy food. It tastes gross."

"Healthy food doesn't have to taste bad, but I have

no idea how to cook it." Alabama's attempt at lasagna had proved to be pretty gross. Tonight's meal she hoped would be better. The man at the grocery store said it was foolproof, even to someone who screwed up boiling water.

"Anything you cook I'm sure will be better than Miss Teresa."

Alabama raised her finger to her lips. "Shhhh. She should be back any second." It was never in good taste to speak badly of anyone in their own home.

As soon as Wyoming saw Sky, he started to kick out his legs and wiggle his fingers. "Ky," he exclaimed.

"Someone is happy to see you." Alabama bent over and handed the baby to Sky. She'd been in awe at how much her son had taken to the girls in such a short period of time, but then again, Wyoming had been going from place to place to place for months. He'd been handed off to one person after the other. He'd gotten used to strangers, and his trust level was through the roof.

Where Alabama was the complete opposite.

Sky quickly zipped up her coat and handed her goodie bag off to her sister. "Hey there, little man."

"She's such a good little helper," Teresa said, holding out a plastic container. "But he might be a little too heavy for her to handle all the way back to the car. If I were you, I'd carry him."

"I can—"

"You're not me." Alabama cut Sky off. While she

was sure Sky could handle the condescending woman, Alabama needed to gain some confidence, and this seemed like the perfect place. "And Sky is perfectly capable of carrying *my* son to the car, thank you." She glanced down at Sky, who smiled wildly. "Are you ready?"

"Yes, ma'am," Sky said as she walked through the open door.

Alabama had to admit that was the most fun she'd had in a year.

DAKOTA SNAPPED a picture of Wyoming's birth certificate as well as the few pieces of mail he'd found in the drawer by the front door of the tiny house. The address on Alabama's car insurance matched the address in upstate New York she'd given him as her last known address.

After a simple Google search, Dakota had found that the duplex had been owned by the same family for twenty years. They rented out both sides. Trish had done a deep dive into the rental records, and it turns out that on paper, it appeared that Alabama did indeed live there. However, Trish saw some discrepancies and was doing a more extensive search, but it had to be done without triggering an alert with the underground.

Or, whoever Alabama was running from.

"Have you thought about trying to contact Chauncey?" Clayton asked as he jumped from the steps of the tiny house and tossed a stick for Buster to chase after, creating a ton of foot traffic in the snow so that Alabama wouldn't be suspicious when she returned.

"I have." Dakota zipped up his coat and adjusted his hat over his ears. Chauncey worked with the underground, and while he was more of a ghost, Dakota and Clayton had a few ways to reach him. "But if there is a bear, I don't want to poke it."

"She's taking care of your kids. If it were me, I'd be doing the same thing."

Dakota bent over and snagged the stick that Buster dropped at his feet. He tossed it as far as he could on the other side of the tiny house. "That's really funny coming from a man who was raised by a hooker and spent most of his life defending them."

"Ah, but it was almost always the prostitute that needed protecting from the paying customer."

"True that." Dakota couldn't argue that point. "On the one hand, I really want to know who her abuser was." He held up his hand. "If she had an abuser, because we don't know that for a fact."

"Either way, you need some information, and Chauncey might be better equipped to find it than us without poking that bear."

"I'll put a call into him first thing in the morning."

"Well, I better get going. Sage is about out of her

mind with this morning sickness stuff, then add in my wild one-year-old daughter, and I think Sage is about ready to hit the underground herself."

"Lunar never had morning sickness, but she felt the same way with River. She's still a little ball of energy. I can't keep up half the time."

"Lunar was a good woman, and we all miss her." Clayton tossed the stick for Buster one last time. "But don't you think it's time to start putting yourself out there?"

"Let's not go down the dating road. My daughters are making me crazy with it as it is. They even have a list of potential girlfriends for me."

Clayton laughed. "They've shown it to Sage."

"Fucking wonderful." Dakota waggled his finger. "And don't you go adding fuel to the fire. I've got enough on my plate raising two girls by myself along with my job. Add in training a new nanny who might be on the run—"

"A hot new nanny," Clayton said with a grin. "Who happens to be single."

"She's not even thirty. Too young for my blood."

"Oh please, my wife is fifteen years younger than me, so don't give me that bullshit. And if you're going to try the kid card, I'm calling you on that too."

"It's both of those things and the fact she's on the run. I don't need that in my life, or my girls."

Clayton nodded. "I'll give you that; only you invited that crap into your life when you offered her the job as nanny before doing the proper background check."

"Come on. Tell me you would have done anything differently than I have."

Clayton arched a brow. "Just admit that besides wanting to protect her that you've found yourself attracted to a woman for the first time since Lunar died."

"That's not true. I find a lot of women attractive."

"That's not what I meant, and you know it." Clayton pulled his keys from his pocket and tossed them in the air. "It's getting late, so I better get on home."

"I'll see you tomorrow at the office." Dakota pushed his fingers into his mouth and whistled.

Buster came running as if he were being chased by a pack of wild wolves.

"You're a good boy." He kicked his boots against the side of the porch, making sure he got off as much snow as possible before entering the house. Once inside, he fed Buster and poured himself a nice glass of Merlot. He settled down in front of the fireplace with his laptop and tried to work instead of staring out the window, waiting for his girls and Alabama to return home. He didn't want to admit that Clayton was right about how much she'd gotten under his skin. Months before Lunar died, he swore to her that he'd keep an open mind about falling in love someday in the future; he just never believed he'd ever find a woman that gave him butterflies in his stomach again.

Never in a million years did he think a woman could keep him up at night thinking about what it would be like to feel her skin under his touch. To hear her soft moans—nope—he needed to stop that train of thought. Simply put, he hadn't had sex in three years. He was horny. He should go out and find himself a booty call. A friend with benefits. A woman who wouldn't expect anything from him, not even a kiss goodbye, much less a phone call the next day.

He shivered at the thought. He'd never been a one-night stand or casual relationship kind of man. He'd had two girlfriends his entire life. His high school sweetheart whom he dated for four years. She couldn't handle it when he went off to the military. Right after boot camp, he'd met Lunar. It was love at first sight, and they married six months later.

His phone buzzed. He glanced at the screen.

Teresa: I met your new nanny. She seems a little terse, but the girls like her.

Dakota rolled his eyes. He'd told Teresa a dozen times he thought she was a nice woman but didn't have time for dating. He'd have to be more firm.

But not in a text.

For now, he'd ignore.

Only, his phone continued to ding.

Teresa: She also seemed stressed, handling her little boy with your girls. I think it might be too much for her. I can help out this week. Actually, I told you I was more than happy to watch your girls before and after school.

He let out a long breath. "Thanks, but no thanks."

Teresa: I thought I'd stop by tomorrow evening with some food. We can talk then.

Shit. He needed to do this now.

Dakota: Alabama is perfectly capable, and tomorrow isn't good. I appreciate the offer, but we're all good.

Teresa: Valentine's Day is coming up. We should get both families together. It's on a Saturday.

Dakota: I'm busy with the girls and Alabama and her son, but thanks. Gotta run.

Hopefully, that would put an end to Teresa and her constant showing up when she wasn't wanted.

Headlights cut through the dark night. His heart pounded in excitement while he watched Alabama pull into the driveway. He jumped from his chair and raced through the house toward the garage. They were expecting six inches of snow. Tapping the garage door opener, he slipped on his boots and stepped into the cold night. "Hey," he called. "Park inside."

"What? Why?" She held a sleeping baby in her arms.

"I'll take care of your car. You can go put him down in the in-law apartment. I set up a crib back there for you earlier." He took the keys from her hands.

"Why would you do that?" Alabama asked with a puzzled expression.

"So he has a comfortable place to nap when you're working." He pulled both his girls in for a hug. "Once I park the car, you two can help me unload the groceries, and I have a treat for supper."

"I bought stuff to make a rice and chicken dish. The guy at the grocery store said anyone can do it."

"I'm sure it will be good to make tomorrow night. Tonight, my specialty."

"Daddy made shepherd's pie," Sky said as she grabbed a couple of bags. "Come on, Miss Alabama. I'll help you put him down."

"This isn't necessary. This is your family time. I'm sure the other nannies you've had didn't stay for dinner. I'll just go put him down in the tiny house and call it a night."

He reached out and curled his fingers around her biceps. "I've never had a nanny who lived in my back-yard who also had a little boy who stole my kids', as well as my own, heart. Besides, what are you going to eat? Some frozen microwave dinner? I won't hear of it, and when that little fella wakes up, he's going to want to try my shepherd's pie. So, we're not taking no for an answer, are we, girls?"

"We are not!" River exclaimed as she yanked a few bags from the back seat. "Only I think some of these groceries aren't ours but go in the tiny house."

"We'll sort them out inside, and I'll trek them over

before we sit down. Now, skedaddle because this old man is freezing."

Both his girls took off running. However, Alabama didn't budge. She just stood there, swaying back and forth, patting Wyoming's back.

"Don't use your girls to manipulate me," she said with a shaky tone.

He hated that she was afraid of him, but at least she was speaking her mind. "I'm sorry. And you're right. I did do that. But we like having you around, and I enjoy the adult conversation."

"You have adult conversation every day at work."

"That's true. How about I just want to have dinner with you and my girls. Please? Will you join us? Like I said, the crib—"

"Why would you do that?"

He cocked his head. "Excuse me?

"Are you expecting me to move in?"

"No." He glanced around. "The girls go back to school on Monday. That reduces your hours. How do you feel about housework?"

"What does that have to do with this conversation?"

"I fired my cleaning service, so if you want that job too, it's yours. I'd also rather you live in the in-law apartment. Not the tiny house. It will be easier for you, and your son. It's roomier, and you won't have to dredge across the yard in the cold. I can rent the tiny house to someone else at some point. I can have some buddies of mine move you in tomorrow. Sound good?"

"More work and money sounds great. But I don't want to live with you, and I don't like how you're basically telling me what to do."

He shivered. "You won't be living with me. The apartment has its own entrance." He pointed toward the back door. "And also an entrance in the house. You can use the garage and when I travel, you can just keep the doors open so if the girls need you, they can find you. That way, you're not moving back and forth all the time. It would be more stable for Wyoming in the long run." If Clayton were here, he'd have a fucking field day with what Dakota just offered. Worst part was that Dakota hadn't even planned on doing it. It just flew from his mouth like word vomit.

"You just have all the answers, don't you?"

"I'm just trying to make both our lives easier. Now if you don't mind, I'm turning blue." Without waiting for her to answer, he slipped into the driver's side, slamming his knees against the dash. "Fuck," he mumbled as he pushed the seat back. He turned the key and made a mental note to himself that he needed to get her car serviced.

Hell, he should probably trade her car in for a new one, all in the name of keeping his girls safe.

For now, she would be driving his SUV.

He dropped his head to the steering wheel. He'd gone and lost his fucking mind.

Bang!

Pop!

"What the fuck?" He leaped from the vehicle, reaching for his weapon, only he'd left it in the house.

The sound of tires spinning out of control over wet pavement filled the night air. He ducked behind the car door and tried to read the license plate off the white pickup as it sped by. He only got a partial plate number, but he didn't need it to know who the driver was.

He raced into the house to find Alabama had both girls and her son curled up in the back corner of the kitchen.

"Daddy!" River raced into his arms. "Are you okay?"

"Yup. Everyone in here okay?" He snagged his cell from the table and quickly texted the Brotherhood. He needed to get ahead of this situation with Candice and her boyfriend, Chad, before it blew out of control and hurt someone he cared about.

"Yes, just scared," Sky said. "Was that gunfire?"

Dakota didn't want to alarm his family, but he didn't want to lie to them either. "It could have been hunters. We've heard them too close to the house before. That's why Daddy doesn't let you go out site in the backyard."

"It sounded too close for that," Sky said.

His daughter was right.

"And you know who we saw in town today?" River asked but didn't wait for him to respond. "Candice. She cornered Alabama right outside of the grocery store. I didn't hear what she said, but she looked awfully mad. Then, she and her boyfriend, Chad, drove by Miss Teresa's house as if they were following us. I bet he shot at us." Leave it to his six-year-old daughter to put all the pieces together.

"You know how I feel about jumping to conclusions." Dakota set River down and looked over his daughters up and down. "But it's a good thing I called my boss and the local police to come out here and check on things." He should have let the police deal with Candice from the beginning. Even her grandfather had agreed what she'd done had been inexcusable, and ever since she started hanging out with Chad, she'd been crossing the line. "I saw that Alabama brought home some cookies. Why don't you two girls set out a plate full and some milk." Kneeling in front of Alabama, he reached out and ran a hand over Wyoming's head. "Take this little guy with you." He sat on the floor and drew a very pale Alabama into his arms. He tucked her hair behind her shoulders and kissed her temple. "Breathe in through your nose, counting to five, and then let it out slowly, counting backwards."

She coughed and gagged at her first attempt, but

her second and third she got the hang of the breathing exercise.

The sound of gunfire was certainly cause for concern, but this seemed over the top considering she'd been inside.

That said, it drove the idea home that she was on the run from something horrible.

Thankfully, her horrible hadn't found her. But he would protect and keep her safe from Candice and her crazy-ass boyfriend.

"That's it," he whispered, running his hands up and down her arms.

"Did someone actually shoot at you?" she asked with a shaky voice.

"I don't believe so."

"Then what happened?" She tilted her head and stared at him with wide, frightened eyes.

"I think my ex-nanny has a screw loose, and her boyfriend is a jackass, and they tried to scare us." He needed Alabama to understand that it wasn't whatever she was running from that created this problem. She and her son weren't in danger from their past.

"Well, it worked." Abruptly, Alabama pushed away and jumped to her feet. "I'm sorry. I don't know what's gotten into me. I'll just get Wyoming, and we'll get out of your hair."

He took her by the forearms. "Alabama, you're not going anywhere and because of what just happened, that's more reason for you to move into my in-law apartment." He cupped her chin. "I'm not going to let anyone hurt you. Not anyone from your past. And certainly not my ex-nanny and her stupid boyfriend." Before she could say another word, he kissed her plump lips. Heat flowed through his body, scorching his skin. Every nerve ending burst into flames. It was as if he'd been transported back into the seventh grade and he was experiencing his very first kiss again.

She slammed her hand on his chest. "What do you know about my past?"

"I know you're running from something."

"You don't know anything about me or my past." She shook out her hands. "Something needs to be done about Candice, or I'm going to have to take my son and leave."

"Don't worry. The police and the man I work for are already on it." Out of the corner of his eye, he saw a patrol car roll into the driveway. "This is the best place for you to stop running. I can keep you safe. But you have to tell me who you're hiding from and why."

An officer tapped at the front door.

"This conversation isn't over." Dakota would get her to open up. He had to.

CHAPTER 4

DAKOTA PUSHED OPENED the precinct doors. The dry heat smacked his skin with vengeance.

"Keep a cool head." Maddog slapped his back.

"Right. Because you'd be able to do that if some idiot took a couple of shots at your family." Normally, Dakota could keep his temper in check. He wasn't sure if it was because of what Chad may have done, or if was because he'd kissed Alabama when he knew damn well he shouldn't have.

Not to mention she was more focused on his comment about her past.

Rookie mistake.

Of course, if he was being honest with himself, the fact she didn't even acknowledge the kiss is what sent him over the edge.

"You need to keep it together inside here, or Hank

will have your head," Maddog said in a stern fatherly voice. "You need to let the locals handle this."

"As long as they do it right, I will." Dakota let out a puff of air as he strode toward the reception desk.

"Hey, Dakota," Archie, the desk officer, said. "You can go right back to interrogation two. Wilson is waiting for you."

"Thanks." For the most part, the Brotherhood Protectors had a decent relationship with the local police department. They often had to work in tandem, but there were times they butted heads.

He hoped this wasn't one of those times.

Just as they rounded the corner, Maddog grabbed his forearm. "You need to calm the fuck down."

"You need to back the fuck off."

Maddog shook his head. "Listen to me, man. We're being given a courtesy here. If you want answers, don't act like a raging lunatic."

"Trust me. Once I walk into that room, I will be nothing but professional. Until then, let me be an asshole." Dakota absolutely knew he needed to act as if it hadn't been him and his family someone took a shot at.

"All right." Maddog held up his hand.

Dakota continued down the hallway, opening and closing his fists. The closer he got to the interrogation room, the faster his heart pounded.

Detective Wilson leaned against the wall with his arms folded. "You two got here fast."

"We came as soon as we heard you picked him up," Maddog said. "We were told he was picked up with a handgun in his possession."

"That is correct." Wilson pushed from the wall. "The handgun had been fired, and Chad does have gun residue on his hands." Wilson wedged a toothpick into his mouth. "But he said he was at the firing range earlier today, and that alibi does pan out."

"What time was he there?" Dakota asked.

"Eleven this morning until one in the afternoon," Wilson said. "He admits to following your friend from the grocery store to Teresa Babcock's place, but says he never drove by your place."

"Did he say why he followed Alabama?" Dakota stepped sideways and peered through the small window into the interrogation room. Chad leaned back in the metal chair as if he didn't have a care in the world. He certainly didn't appear to be too worried by the situation.

"He said his girlfriend asked him to because she wanted to make sure Sky and River were safe. He said she doesn't trust your new nanny because she's a liar." Wilson shifted the toothpick to the other side of his mouth. "We sent an officer to her house, but she's not there. As of right now, we have no idea where she is."

Dakota didn't like the sound of that. He pulled out his cell.

Dakota: Everything okay?

71

Alabama: Yes. Girls are asleep. Your friends have me all moved in.

Dakota: Clayton and Viper still there?

Alabama: Yes. They said they wanted to wait for you. I set them up in your family room with some beer, chips, and dip. Wyoming and I are going to bed.

Dakota: Okay. I'll be home in an hour or less. If you're awake, leave the light on by your door. I'd like to talk to you.

He tucked his phone in his back pocket. No need to wait for her to respond now. He'd know his answer when he returned to the house.

"Have you checked with her grandfather?" Maddog asked.

"We have, and he hasn't heard from her since Dakota fired her. I guess she and the old man had words, and she decided she was better off on her own," Wilson said. "When we pressed Chad where she might be, he informed us that they got into a fight, and he left her in town and hasn't spoken to her since."

"What was the fight about?" Dakota asked.

"Chad said she wanted him to keep following Alabama, but he didn't want to. He wanted to go drinking, which is where we picked him up, and the bartender said he'd been there since an hour before you called the locals." Wilson popped out the tooth-pick and waggled it in the air. "But you should know, he let Candice take his pickup."

"Wait a second," Maddog said. "You're telling us that basically there is no way in hell Chad shot at Dakota and his family."

"It appears that way," Wilson said. "But based on what you've said and something else we found out, Candice might have."

"What else have you found out?" Dakota asked.

"Right before I learned you two had arrived, Chad told me that Candice had heard from a waitress friend from the Eagle Rock Diner that they didn't hire your new nanny, Alabama, because they couldn't find enough about her on the internet, and nothing really came back on a background check. So, Candice asked Chad's father to do some digging."

Fuck. Wilmot Hooker knew a lot of bad people in high places, and if there was something to uncover in Alabama's past, Wilmot would be able to do it.

That was a bear in hibernation that didn't awakening.

"There's nothing to find there, trust me. My organization has done serious digging." Dakota normally wouldn't lie to the cops, but he didn't want them to go poking around in Alabama's background. "She checks out. No red flags of any kind."

"Good to know," Wilson said. "How long was Candice an employee of yours?"

"Five months," Dakota said. In the beginning, she'd been an attentive nanny. He'd trusted his girls were in good hands, and until a couple of weeks ago, that had been the case. "But she'd been a part-time babysitter for me for two years, and I'd never had a problem with her before."

"After her mother died, she'd been in and out of trouble," Wilson said. "Nothing major, but her last year in high school, she'd been picked up for possession a couple of times."

"I knew that when I hired her." Dakota had a soft spot for Candice's grandfather as well as wanting to give the young woman a chance at turning her life around before she started making bad choices she couldn't recover from.

She still had that opportunity.

He hoped.

"You still haven't told me anything that says Candice is the one who shot at me." Dakota didn't want to believe that Candice would go that far, but he had to be realistic about the situation, especially since his girls were involved.

As well as Alabama and her son.

"She has Chad's gun."

ALABAMA FLICKED the light switch by the door to the in-law apartment five times before deciding to shut it off and head to the kitchen for a glass of wine. The last text from Dakota indicated he'd be home in the next twenty minutes.

Or less.

While she wanted to express her dislike of the new living situation, she also wanted to let him know she appreciated his diligence in making sure her son was safe. She did want him to know she truly valued how he went out of his way to help her and her kid.

She also wanted to know what happened with Candice and her boyfriend. Alabama needed to know that they were her only threat and that the local police and the Brotherhood Protectors would be taking care of that situation.

Otherwise, she would be on the road before morning.

"Is everything okay?" Viper asked, standing in the middle of the hallway.

Alabama jumped. "Shit. You scared the crap out of me." She smoothed down the front of her flannel pajama bottoms before checking her top to make sure all the buttons were securely fastened.

"Sorry." Viper held up his phone. "Dakota texted, and he's about five minutes out."

"Where's Clayton?" She scurried past Viper and snagged one of the stemless wine glasses and filled it with red wine. She took a big gulp. For the last hour, she'd counted her cash and looked online for places to move.

Florida seemed like an option.

Or maybe Texas.

It would have been a lot easier to sneak out in the

middle of the night had Dakota not insisted she move into the main house. Her heart dropped like a brick into her gut. Leaving the girls would be difficult. She hated hurting them, but what choice did she have?

"He's outside checking the perimeter," Viper said. "Unfortunately, while Chad is in custody, we still have no idea where Candice is."

Alabama had to appreciate how honest Dakota and all his co-workers have been regarding the situation, but she still didn't trust them, and she worried about his comment about her past. Her true identity had to remain a secret. If it didn't, she and her son were as good as dead.

Headlights cut through the dark night. The slight hum of the garage door opener tickled her ears. What Dakota had to say would be the deciding factor on whether or not she left tonight or toughed it out for a little while longer.

The back door opened, and she heard both Dakota and Clayton enter the house.

"I'm so glad you're awake," Dakota said as he pulled down a glass and poured himself some wine. He held up the bottle, but both his buddies shook their heads. "I've got some good news."

"We'll get Maddog to fill us in," Clayton said. "We'll see you tomorrow."

"Thanks for helping out." Dakota rested his hand on the small of Alabama's back. "Why don't we go sit in front of the fireplace."

She'd rather take her wine to bed but decided she shouldn't be rude. She curled up on the far side of the sofa, tucking her feet under her butt. Staring at the crackling fire, she let out a slow breath. "So, what's the good news?"

"Well, it's good and bad news, depending on how you look at it." He poked at the fire before joining her on the sofa. "We found Candice." He positioned himself closer to the center and a little too close to her.

"Is that the good news or the bad news?" she asked, feeling the heat from his body coat her skin like a warm, fuzzy blanket. She hated the way he reminded her that she was indeed a woman who still craved the closeness of a man.

And damn, Dakota was all man.

"It's good because the police have taken her into the station for questioning, and once she's released, we've got constant eyes on her, so we'll know where she is and what she's doing at all times."

"Making her still being on the streets and having an axe to grind with me, the bad news," Alabama said. When she'd left the underground, they told her to blend in. To make sure she didn't draw attention to herself.

Well, she certainly screwed that up.

He nodded. "But, after speaking with her, even though she hasn't admitted to what she's done, I've known her a long time, and she'd never hurt my girls. I can guarantee all she wanted to do was scare you."

"She's done a damn good job of that."

"And I think she wants to make you quit so I'll have to hire her back, which is childish and will never happen." He raised his glass to his lips and sipped.

"I don't know about that," she said softly. "I really like it here, and I've become attached to your girls, but this isn't the kind of environment I want to raise my son in."

He rested his arm on the back of the sofa and arched a brow. "What happened today isn't something that happens regularly. As a matter of fact, I can honestly say that it's never happened in my personal life, ever."

She opened her mouth to remind him of his military past, but he pressed his index finger over her lips.

"In my line of work, I've dealt with some really bad people. Murderers. Psychopaths. I've been on the front line of war, and I've been in street fights. I've seen it all, and Candice isn't out to hurt anyone. She's misguided, and unfortunately Chad has been known to make some bad decisions, but neither one of them have done anything violent."

If she had a dollar for everyone who couldn't believe Josh would ever lay a finger on anyone, she'd be a millionaire. "You said she's been smoking weed. If she's been doing that, who knows what other drugs she might be taking, and who knows what kind of violence that might lead to. I can't expose my son to that."

He leaned forward and placed his glass on the coffee table. "If I thought this was truly a volatile situation, I'd be sending my children, and you and your son, to a safe house provided by my company." He scooted closer, taking her hand into his and rubbing his thumb over her palm. "Not to sound too arrogant, but I'm really good at my job. I'm also really good at reading people and situations. There are two things I know for sure. First, Candice is angry and she's acting out, but she's got a moral compass, and she won't cross it. And second, you're not considering quitting because of her. But I want you to know, whatever, or whoever, you're running from, you are safe here. No one will hurt you, or your son, while you are living on my land."

She swallowed her gasp. "Excuse me?" She jerked her hand back.

He stood and strolled across the room. Lifting a frame from the mantel, he turned, showing off an image of him and a beautiful dark-haired woman holding a baby while he carried another child on his shoulders with a proud smile. "I'm sorry. I'm not as good at this as my late wife, Lunar, would have been.

This was her area of expertise. She's probably yelling at me from heaven right now for fucking this all up."

"I really have no idea what you're talking about." Alabama untucked her legs and set her feet on the floor, ready to race off to her room. "I won't leave you without a nanny, but I think—"

"I can't let you leave."

"That's not your choice," she said with a shaky voice. It shouldn't be hard to dig her heels in and stand her ground, but Josh had really done a number on her, and she'd allowed him to take away all her power.

She wasn't going to do it again.

He rubbed his temples. "I know I can't make you stay, but it's better for you if you do. I can protect you and your son from your past."

She bolted upright. "You keep bringing up my past. What the hell do you think you know?"

"Nothing, but if you choose to tell me, it will make it easier for me to make sure *he* never lays a hand on you or Wyoming again."

"Well, you have some nerve," she said, doing her best to sound insulted instead of utterly terrified. "I don't know who you think you are, but—"

"Lunar worked with the underground and a man by the name of Chauncey. They created new identities and helped battered women disappear. Occasionally, I provided services to ensure safe passage. It was my wife's life work."

"Chauncey?" Tears burned at Alabama's eyes. She couldn't stand to listen to this anymore. She turned on her heels, but he grabbed her by the forearms and spun her around.

"You know him?"

"No." She squeezed her eyes shut.

"I don't believe you," he said sternly. "Look at me."

She blinked. "I don't know what you're talking about."

"I think you do. You see, when Lunar was five, her mom was beaten so badly by her father that she was unrecognizable. My wife's childhood was riddled with the kind of pain that never goes away. When I first started working with her, I thought it would be better to let the system work and put these asshole men in prison. Only, I learned very quickly our system is fucked and often men like Lunar's father weren't even given a slap on the wrist. When I met my wife, she was just starting to put the pieces of her life together, and I can see in your eyes, what I saw in hers. I know that look. I'm not judging you or your decisions. If anything, I commend you for getting out. You have a safe haven here for as long as you want it, but I'd like to know what and who you're running from."

"Let go of me," she said behind gritted teeth. Her entire body shook. Every slap, punch, and kick she'd endured at the hands of Josh came down on her mind at once. The crippling fear nearly brought her to her knees. "You're way off base."

He tugged her closer.

She resisted, but he didn't let go.

Oddly, she didn't feel threatened.

She felt cared for.

And that scared her on a different level.

"I'm right on target." He took her chin with his thumb and forefinger. "Running from your husband?"

She gasped but quickly snapped her mouth shut. Saying anything to him would be her kiss of death.

"Look. The only way I can make sure you will always be safe is to know who you're running from. I've done some poking, but I don't want to do a deep probe. I do that, and I might just end up tipping him off."

"You've been spying on me? How dare you. Who the hell do you think you are?" Her insides rattled like a snake's tail, fast and hard.

"I'm your employer, for starters. I have the right to know who is taking care of my kids," he said in a calm voice. His hands ran up and down her arms in a warm and caring gesture. He had an uncanny way of making her feel safe. She used to think Josh made her feel that way, but it was a false sense of caring. In reality, all she ever felt for Josh was fear.

Gently, Dakota took cupped her chin. "Believe

me, I'm on your side. Are you running from your husband?"

"Yes." She shouldn't tell him anything, but if his wife's friend was the same man who recommended Eagle Rock, Montana, and specifically showed her the tiny house rental, then she knew she had to trust Dakota, even if she didn't want to.

"Did he hurt Wyoming?"

"No. Not really."

"What the hell does not really mean?" Dakota asked with a tight jaw.

"Josh, my husband, beat me for the last time on the day Wyoming was born. He was a month early because of that beating." Her breath came in short, choppy pants. Rage filled her heart as if she were the keeper of hell. "The nurse at the hospital knew someone at the underground and set me up. The night before I was to be released, I disappeared. I went from one hiding place to the next until I was no longer featured on the national news."

"National?" he asked with a curved brow. "Why would you make the national news regarding your disappearance unless someone thought you were dead?"

"I doubt anyone thinks I'm dead, and I know my husband doesn't want to put that in anyone's head. He'd prefer the world see me as this rotten bitch who stole his kid."

"Who's your husband?" Dakota asked.

"Josh Brolin."

"You've got to be fucking kidding me." Dakota dropped his hands to his sides. "The son of one of the most notorious criminals in the United States? You're Amanda Brolin?"

"In the flesh."

CHAPTER 5

FOR SOME STRANGE REASON, Alabama felt as if the weight of the world had just been lifted from her shoulders. It was as if she said Josh's name and a hundred pounds dropped off her body.

"Fuck," Dakota muttered as he entered the family room carrying a tray of food. "He's a fucking monster."

"You don't have to tell me that." Just having one person know her true identity both horrified her and comforted her in ways she couldn't describe, much less explain.

Dakota set a plate with a grilled cheese sandwich on the coffee table before pouring two more glasses of wine. He settled back on the sofa while he munched on his snack and sipped his beverage.

"You didn't expect me to drop that big of a bomb now, did you?" Alabama said with a long sigh. She leaned back, resting her head on the back of the sofa, and stared at the ceiling. When she'd first met Josh, she had to admit his family name gave her pause, but his charm melted all that away in a matter of seconds. Besides, during their dating phase, Josh didn't spend a lot of time with his father, or the family business.

Or, at least that's what she thought.

During their engagement, she learned otherwise. Looking back, she saw all the signs, but she chose to ignore them.

"No, I can't say that I did," he admitted. "I knew whoever you were hiding from had to be an asshole; I just never expected him to be a powerful asshole with government officials in his back pocket."

"Have you told your buddies yet?" she asked with a heavy dose of sarcasm. She knew he would, eventually, but she figured as soon as that happened, she'd need to be on the run again. But at least she knew she'd be able to get in contact with the underground since he knew Chauncey, and maybe, just maybe, Chauncey might be able to work some magic and get her and her son another new identity in a new city and state.

Maybe they could move her out of the country.

"Not yet and when the time comes, I'll just be having a conversation with my boss Hank and maybe my buddy Clayton. He and his wife run a few charities for the homeless and for prostitutes, but they also do work with battered women and children.

They will have a lot of connections and will also know how to make sure we keep your identity and whereabouts under wraps."

"I don't like anyone knowing who I am," she said.

"I don't plan on telling anyone who you are unless my boss thinks I should. Otherwise, they will help me navigate this without that knowledge. But it depends on a lot of things. One of them being Chauncey, if I ever hear back from him."

"When I got to him, he thought my name was Alice."

"Chauncy had to know who you were, or he wouldn't have sent you to me." Dakota chuckled. "In all the years I've known Chauncey, he's never put anyone in my backyard. He didn't send you here with the idea that no one would figure out that you were on the run. There are too many men and women working for the Brotherhood Protectors in this area. We're a way too suspicious group. Chauncey sent you here on purpose."

"Then why didn't he just call and tell you that?"

"Because that could send up a red flag with anyone who might be looking for you, including the FBI."

"They think I kidnapped my own son," she said softly.

"Among other things."

"I don't want to know." She tossed her forearm over her eyes and groaned. "When my water broke,

Josh went and smashed my car, put me in it, and called the first responders. He wanted everyone to believe I was in a car accident. No one believed him, but no one did anything because half the police department is terrified of him and his father."

"They are horrible people." He tugged at her hand, forcing her to sit up. "I need you to walk me through what happened from the time you went underground —specifically, who knew your true identity."

"Why is that important?"

"When did you first meet Chauncey?" he asked, avoiding her question. He'd answer that eventually.

"A couple of months ago," she said. "When I landed in San Diego."

"How long where you there?"

"Just a couple of weeks. It was my last stop and really just to help me get out in the world."

"And that's the problem." Dakota took his wine glass, stood, and started to pace in front of the fireplace. "The way the underground works with a high-profile case such as yours is that each time they move you, they give you a burn identity. Each new group of volunteers you work with think that burn identity is actually your real identity. Your narrative stays the same, meaning if it was your husband who abused you and you ran off right after childbirth, that doesn't change, but you were never Amanda Brolin, not since that first initial run. So, even Chauncey shouldn't have known who you were."

"I understand that. When I flew to San Diego, it was in part to test the identity, but they had me go back to Albany, New York, and fly from there to make my story plausible, which was terrifying. I hated being so close to Manhattan."

"I can imagine," he said. "But tell me, did you meet Chauncey right away, or did that happen right before you came here?"

"I met him about three or four days before I got on the road, but that still doesn't mean anything to me. I don't understand where you are going with all this."

"Where did Chauncey tell you to go?"

"He recommended this area over the places I was looking at in Wyoming. He showed me your rental, but it wasn't the only one.

"But did he push in that direction? Did he say anything about knowing the area? Or it being quiet and remote, and it would be easy for you to blend in living in that tiny house?"

"Yeah. Actually, he did." Alabama leaned forward and rubbed her temples. "Obviously, everyone at the hospital in Manhattan knew who I was even if you couldn't tell by looking at me. It was the first time Josh had ever hit me in the face." Her eyes burned from the tears flowing like a raging river. She couldn't stop them if she tried. "I remember lying on the kitchen floor curled up in a little ball as he kicked and hit me, laughing at me, telling me the first thing our baby was going to see was how hideous his mother was."

"Fucking bastard," Dakota muttered. He knelt in front of her and wrapped his strong, protective arms around her shaking body.

"I should have gotten out sooner. Josh could have killed Wyoming."

"You can should have, could have all day long. The fact is, you did get out. You and Wyoming are safe." He lifted her chin and tenderly wiped her tears away.

She searched his gaze for that sign that said he was a bad man. For that hint of something that told her trusting him was a mistake.

But all she saw was a kind soul.

"I was able to leave Josh thanks to a nurse who, once she realized the police weren't going to arrest my husband, or even slap his wrist, found a way to sneak me and my son out and sent me to a shelter in New Jersey."

"Anyone there know you?" He sat on the sofa next to her, pulling her head to his chest. His fingers glided through her hair, occasionally tickling the skin on her shoulders and arms.

"The nurse had a friend who worked there. I spent two nights there while she got me a fake ID and sent me underground in Pennsylvania. I stayed Alice for a couple of months, and I went from one shelter to the next until I was then moved to Virginia where I worked in a soup kitchen with a new identity. It went on like that until I ended up in San Diego."

"So, to your knowledge, the only people who knew your real identity was the nurse and the person in New Jersey?"

"After New Jersey and until now, I've never uttered my real name," she said. "However, when I landed in San Diego, the plan had been for me to head to Wyoming, but Chauncey also talked me out of that plan. He said my kid's name would draw attention to us, and he really thought I'd have better luck finding a job here." She brushed her hair from her face and stiffened her spine. That was enough crying on her boss' shoulder for one day.

"When did Chauncey recommend the change?"

"The morning I left," she admitted.

"I think Chauncey either knew there was a breakdown in privacy and someone in the underground was talking. Or he just knew who you were and was being super cautious, knowing that I would see the signs and would do whatever I could to protect you."

"He said I would never see or hear from him again under any circumstance."

"Well, he lied because we do have a way of contacting him. The question is do we want to do that right now when there is absolutely no reason to believe you are in danger of any kind."

"Except for Candice and her boyfriend."

"Normally, I wouldn't believe in coincidences, but

I don't see a connection. That said, my team is working to make sure there is no way Candice, Chad, or his family has any dealings with your husband or knows anyone in the underground."

"I overheard your friend Clayton and Viper talking about Chad and his family. While I've never heard the name Hooker in any of Josh's dealings, it doesn't mean that Josh's family dealings didn't stretch this far. He now owns nightclubs in Vegas and property in Lake Tahoe." It always amazed Alabama how many people she'd met while married to Josh who enjoyed bending and breaking the laws in the name of getting ahead. Of course, Josh kept her from most of the family business dealings, but the longer she stayed married, the more she realized Josh and his family were nothing more than gangsters.

"The Brotherhood Protectors have worked cases in the past involving members of your husband's organization." Dakota pinched the bridge of his nose. "Specifically, we were hired a couple of years ago to protect Leslie Witcher."

Alabama gasped. Her heart pounded in her chest. Leslie had been her friend. Her confidant. And then one day, she vanished, only to show up months later with enough evidence to take down her own husband and three other people inside the Brolin organization.

They had tried to find incriminating evidence on Josh and his father, but they failed. Before the trial,

Leslie's husband was found murdered, and three months later, Leslie was found dead in a hotel room.

The headline read: *After falsely accusing a half dozen people of espionage, Leslie Witcher commits suicide.*

"Leslie was my friend." Sucking in a deep breath, she leaned over and lifted the wine glass to her lips. She took a good whiff before letting the bold liquid slide down her throat. "She told me she was going to turn her husband in to the Feds. She said she had evidence that proved he was selling intel to foreign governments. I thought she was crazy, and I told her it would get her killed. She said she knew someone who could protect her."

"Shamus," Dakota said. "Leslie knew his wife from college. Shamus set up the entire protection detail, and we all helped gather the intel, but her husband has a fortress built around him. So does yours. No one could find the connection to the foreign governments, but the DEA had enough on him for drug trafficking. They had to act on Hamlin, and Leslie agreed. So, we turned her, and all the evidence she had and that we collected, over to them. It's not one of our more shining moments as an organization, but we did everything we could."

"She didn't commit suicide. I don't care what the medical examiner stated."

"We've always believed she was murdered, and we are still looking into it. My boss doesn't let these things go, and frankly, neither do any of his employees. We take it personally."

"That doesn't make me feel better. How can I be sure I'm safe here if that happened on your watch?"

"For the record, my company wasn't protecting her during the trial. That was the FBI and the DEA. But you're right, we did fail her. We should have done more."

"Everyone failed her, including me."

"No. You didn't. Until recently, you haven't been in a position to do anything but survive, and you were barely doing that."

"I'm still too scared to do anything."

"Right now, the only thing you need to concern yourself with is protecting yourself and your son, which I can help you with. Let the cops deal with Josh, and let me keep on an eye on that for you."

"My husband has so many lawyers, government officials, cops, and federal agents in his back pocket, no one can touch him. His father and grandfather built a huge protective wall around them starting when his father changed his name from Gorgivani to Brolin, which was his grandmother's maiden name."

"His father did legitimize many businesses, and for a decade, he had the world snowed that his family turned over a new leaf," Dakota said. "But that quickly changed when your husband started running things and started showing his true colors, but the

Feds haven't been able to gather anything of substance to arrest him on."

"I'm very aware of that." She rubbed the side of her stomach, remembering the head blow and how she prayed her husband's pointed expensive shoes didn't kill her unborn child. Every time he kicked her, he'd laugh and tell her how many things he'd gotten away with.

The money laundering.

The corporate espionage.

The selling of technology to foreign countries.

The killing of her only friend.

Her husband's business wasn't typical mafia. Not in the terms of what you saw in the movies. But shakedowns did happen.

And so did murders.

Her husband would do whatever it took to get what he wanted. He had no control, something his late father used to tell him would end up being his demise.

Thus far, his father had been wrong.

"You're a smart woman. What can you tell me about your husband's business dealings? You had to have seen something. Know something."

Shame and rage twisted her gut. She should know more than she did, but she was too busy letting herself die one punch at a time. Instead of being a whole person, she buried her head in the sand. "I know he was a bad man. I know he stole from his own companies. I know he stole from other companies and sold to terrorists. I just can't prove any of it." With as much dignity as she could muster, she stood. "I'm not as smart as you think I am; otherwise, I would have never ended up with such a monster."

"ALABAMA, WAIT." Dakota raced through the house toward the in-law apartment. "I didn't mean it like that." How could he have been so stupid as to imply that her intelligence should have gained her some insight into her husband's criminal dealings when her entire marriage had been about her survival.

"Yes, you did." She paused at the doorway and glanced over her shoulder. "But being smart doesn't mean you're immune to being taken advantage of."

"I know that. The words I used and the way in which I said them didn't come out right. What I meant was that you might not realize that you know something. If we talk things through, we might uncover some important facts."

"My world was very small while I was married to Josh. I had no friends, and he controlled everything I did. When I finally left, I had no idea what to do, or how to do it. The underground had to teach me how to even balance a checkbook. For a woman with a four-year degree, I was totally clueless."

"Not totally," he said. "That's what he wanted you to think, but it wasn't true."

"But it felt that way. Even after I left. For months, I stayed away from watching the news. I didn't want to know what anyone was saying about me, or Josh."

"I'm sure they told you to ignore your old life and not do things like Google yourself."

She nodded. "But it's sometimes impossible not to see it, and about six months ago, I was sitting in a children's clinic. Wyoming had an ear infection. The news came on, and a picture of me flashed across the screen." She reached up and ran a finger through her long blond hair, which he just realized wasn't her natural color.

Not even close.

"Then I saw Josh, and the first thing out of his mouth was how worried he was about his mentally ill wife who kidnapped their newborn son. At that moment, the nurse called us in, and I didn't see any more."

"That's probably—"

She raised her hand. "I don't care what he says about me, as long as my son never has to hear the those lies, and I'm starting to wonder if that will ever be possible."

"I promise you that I will do whatever it takes to keep you and Wyoming safe from that asshole."

"You can't make that promise." Her thick lashes blinked over her soft ocean-blue eyes.

"Alabama, you have to trust me. This isn't my first rodeo when it comes to helping battered women."

She let out a soft chuckle. "I don't trust any man."

"You know I'm not like him. Most men aren't like him."

"Actually, I don't know that," she said, lifting her chin. "You're a very charismatic person. So was Josh. He found my weakness and exploited it. You seem to be finding ways to break down the walls I so carefully constructed, but I obviously didn't use enough grout to keep the tile together."

Dakota wanted to take her into his arms, but he knew right now that would cause her to pull away even more. "I can understand why you're being so guarded."

"I don't think you do," she said. "The day I left San Diego was the first day in almost a year that no one was telling me what to do or where to go. My life was in my hands, or so I thought. But now I find out this Chauncey guy might have sent me here on purpose and you moved me into your house."

"For your safety," he said.

"But you didn't give me a choice."

He took her by the hand and led her into the apartment. He stood in front of the window and glanced out at the snow gently falling to the ground. His wife had few complaints about his personality, but she did have one big one, and that was the way he took charge without thinking about the people around him.

He argued that he constantly thought about everyone around him. That he made those kinds of decisions because as a leader in the military, his men were his responsibility.

Lunar would remind him that his family wasn't in the military with him.

"I'm sorry that you felt strong-armed. I won't do that to you again, and you can always speak your mind with me without fear of being hurt or belittled." He turned. "That said, my job is to protect you—"

"It's not your job."

"You are a tough audience." He let out a puff of air. "I'm good at protecting people, and right now, I want to make sure you and Wyoming have a life where you're not constantly looking over your shoulder."

She plopped herself on the sofa and lifted her feet to the coffee table. "That's never going to happen. For as long as Josh is alive, I've got a target on my back. I can cut my hair and dye it blue, but as long as his heart is beating, my son and I aren't safe."

"Now that I know, you're actually safer because I know what to be on the lookout for." The draw he felt toward Alabama affected him both emotionally and physically. The need to take care of her was so strong it scared him. He hadn't had such intense feelings for anyone other than his children since he'd met Lunar, and he honestly never thought he'd ever meet a woman that made him want to even consider the possibility that he could love again.

He had the kind of romance with Lunar that most people spend their entire life looking for. Finding that kind of love again he figured would never happen.

And yet, there he was, wishing he could lift her into his arms and kiss away her problems.

"I wish I could believe you, but then there is the issue of your girls and putting them in danger, and me being here does exactly that."

Slowly, he closed the gap. He eased himself onto the couch and tapped his index finger on her thigh. "Unfortunately, my job can be dangerous. It's something I've grappled with since I became a father, both in the military and when I resigned my post and began working for Hank and the Brotherhood Protectors. But walking across the street can kill you if you don't look both ways. Besides, if I thought my girls were in any real danger, they wouldn't be here. And frankly, neither would you and Wyoming. And yes, I'd give you a choice on the matter, but I wouldn't like it if you didn't go into hiding."

"I think I actually believe that." She laughed as she shifted to face him. She rested her cheek in the palm of her hand. Her blond hair cascaded over the cushion. The roots were coming in darker, and he couldn't decide which he preferred. The natural brown he'd seen in pictures on the internet and on the news, or the current color combination.

Actually, it didn't matter.

Her hair could be pink, and he'd still like her.

"I haven't been anywhere for more than a month. I'm tired of packing up and moving and changing my name all the time, but all the commotion with Candice, that scared me. And now that you know who I am, and your friends will know, I feel like that's bad for me and my son. They told me never to let anyone know the real me. Once one person knew, then they'd tell someone, and eventually, it would get back to Josh, and this would all be for nothing."

"In most cases, I would absolutely agree with that philosophy, which is why I'm going to be very careful with who I tell anything to, even inside my own organization." He dropped his hand to his lap. "I've asked my team to put a hold on doing any more digging."

She looked at him with wide, scared eyes. "Won't they ask all sorts of questions on why and be suspicious?"

"They still know you're running from something, but they trust my judgment. Soon, though, I will need to take this to my boss. Think of him as a garbage disposable. What goes in gets ground up and doesn't really come out."

"That is the weirdest analogy I've ever heard," she said with some lightness to her tone.

"I've said worse." He reached out and brushed a piece of her hair behind her shoulder. "I really am sorry you felt like I didn't give you any choice about moving into the main house. I know I can come on strong and sometimes even aggressive, but always know it's because I have your best interest at heart."

"Don't take this the wrong way, but Josh used to tell me the same thing."

Dakota groaned as he dropped his head back. "I'm not gaslighting you or trying to manipulate you." He had no idea how to get through to her that he was indeed on her side. All he knew was that words were empty, but actions spoke volumes.

He'd have to keep proving to her that he was one of the good guys.

"Can I ask you a question about him?" Dakota asked.

"I suppose."

"Where'd you meet him?"

"I was in college. My parents had just passed away, and I was in the process of selling off some of their assets when I met him at my lawyer's office, which was also one of his lawyers. I was a hot mess that day, and he was so kind and sweet to me. He helped me navigate the entire process. I felt alone and lost in this world, and he was there to pick up the pieces."

"He met you when you were at your most vulnerable."

She nodded. "He treated me like a princess, always taking me to fancy restaurants and buying me nice things. He supported me finishing my schooling, even though we both agreed I wouldn't work after we got married, and by that time, I was sucked in so deep, I hadn't realized I was a completely different person. I had nowhere to run and no one to run to. Leslie was my only friend. I saw her as a strong woman, and if any of us could get out, it would have been her. So, when she died, more of me did too. And what's worse, I saw what Josh and everyone else in that organization did to her memory by saying she killed herself. She would never do that. I would never endanger my son, and I'm not unstable, like my husband would like the world to believe."

"Men like Josh are masters at manipulation. They can con some of the smartest people in the world given the right circumstances."

"Could he con you?"

Now that was a loaded question, but a fair one. "Josh? Doubtful. At least not at this moment in my life. But someone else? Right after my wife died? Sure. No one is immune to being taken advantage of; only my radar is strong and always on high alert, as yours is now."

"It sucks not being able to trust anyone. I hate thinking that at any moment someone is going to know who I am and go running to Josh and tell him where Wyoming is, and that's what scares me the most. If Josh wants to ruin me or kill me, fine. But Wyoming is an innocent child, and he could turn him into a horrible person. I can't have that."

Dakota ran his thumb over her bottom lip. "Neither can I."

"Why do you care so much about us?"

"That's a good question," he admitted leaning closer. "Ever since you moved in, I haven't been able to think about anything other than this." He pressed his mouth against hers in a slow, but passionate kiss. He started off controlled and tender before parting her plump lips with his tongue. She tasted like strawberries and cream with a hint of sugar.

She rested her hands on his shoulders. He half expected her to either slap him or jerk away.

But she did neither.

He wrapped his arms around her tiny waist and pulled her to his chest. Her breath hitched, and he captured a slight moan as it vibrated in his throat. Everything about her made his heart beat a little faster.

Her body sank into his like the ocean gently lapping against the shore. He wanted to lift her into his arms and carry her to bed, but he knew he couldn't. It was too soon for her.

And for him.

"I should let you get some sleep," he whispered. "I have to go into the office for a few hours tomorrow after the girls go to school. If you want, you can come with me so you're not alone. Or you can hang out with Sage and her one-year-old little girl, Hillary."

"It might be fun for Wyoming to have a playdate," Alabama said.

"I thought it would be good for you to meet Sage. She's Clayton's wife and is about your age. She's also pregnant with their second child."

"She's the one who does all the charity work, right?"

"That's right." Dakota stood, leaving her on the sofa, knowing if he took her into his arms again, he might push to stay all night, and that wouldn't be good. "I'll see you in the morning for breakfast."

"I can't even handle eggs. We should just order out," she said, covering her eyes.

He laughed. "Meet me in the kitchen at seven, and I'll teach you a few things. Trust me, if I can do it, so can you."

"You tried my lasagna; you should know by now I can't."

"And you should know by now I'm not the kind of guy that gives up that easily."

CHAPTER 6

QUIETLY, Alabama closed the door to the apartment and headed back to the main family room. "Both Hillary and Wyoming are sound asleep. River isn't far behind them, and Sky is bright-eyed and bushy-tailed, ready to tend to the babies if one of them wakes up."

"She's going to make a great little babysitter," Sage said as she kicked up her feet on the ottoman near the fireplace and sipped her wine. "She's so good with Hillary, and that child is a holy terror."

"She doesn't get that from me," Clayton said with a playful tone.

Alabama made herself comfortable on the sofa next to Dakota, who looped his arm over the back of the cushions. She tucked her feet under her butt and actually leaned a little closer to the man that had kissed her last night like no one else ever had before.

She could still feel the heat from his lips on hers, and it trickled down her skin all the way to the tips of her toes.

"How on earth do you manage to get Wyoming to be so well behaved?" Sage asked. "No matter what we do, that girl is more stubborn than old man Willie."

"I have no idea. I suppose maybe it's because we've moved around so much." Alabama swallowed. Dakota had told her that Clayton and Sage both knew she had been in the underground but had no idea of her true identity. But Alabama couldn't be sure. Even with light hair, when she looked in the mirror, she could see her old self, so she imagined everyone else could see through the minimal disguise.

"Well, let's just hope they are all well behaved when they become teenagers," Clayton said.

"Amen to that." Dakota raised his glass. "Today, Sky brought home papers for me to sign so she can participate in sex education. I damn near died when she looked me in the eye and said: *Daddy, before you go get all weird and dad-like, I know what having my period is all about; we have supplies stocked up for me when it happens. I also know how babies are made.*"

Alabama stifled her giggle.

"I don't see what's so funny," Dakota said.

"Oh, I wish I had taken a picture of your face when Sky used the words sexual intercourse followed by penis and vagina." Alabama let the laughter bellow from her gut. "I thought his head was going to explode."

"I can't imagine," Clayton said, running a hand down his face and shaking his head. "My daughter won't be having sex. Ever."

"Your daughter is going to marry Wyoming, and they will make beautiful babies, and I will enjoy reminding you that they had *sexual intercourse* to make them." Sage had an edge to her, as if she'd seen the dark underbelly of the world and survived.

However, Alabama had no idea what that might have looked like for Sage.

"I'm not ready for this," Dakota mumbled. "Before I know it, Sky's going to want to go bra shopping." He tapped Alabama on the shoulder. "And that's going to be your job. I can't handle going into Victoria's Secret with my daughter of all people."

If she was still around, she would happily take Sky bra shopping.

God, she wanted to be in this place a year from now. Hell, she could see herself here five years from now, but she had to be realistic about the situation.

Which meant no more kissing Dakota, no matter how much she liked it.

"You, my friend, are going to have to get used to more than just thongs and bras when it comes to your girls. Wait until the boys start knocking at the door," she said, trying to keep the conversation on normal couple things, even though nothing about this was normal.

"They won't be knocking because they will quickly learn that I will answer with a shotgun." Dakota rested his hand on her shoulder. His thumb rubbed a gentle circle over her skin under her ear.

She found herself inching closer. It didn't matter that both Clayton and Sage glanced in her direction with an amused smirk and an arched brow. It didn't matter that she knew deep down that allowing herself even the slightest flirtation with Dakota would end in heartbreak; she needed to feel alive, and that's what he gave her, in spades.

"But what if one of her suitors is someone from the Brotherhood Protectors," Alabama said. "Or a son of a friend of yours? Someone will eventually have to be good enough for her."

"This is why I wish I had a son," Clayton said. "I'd only have one penis to worry about. Not the entire world."

"Oh, my God. That's hilarious," Alabama said. "But you know, raising a son, I have to teach him to not only treat a woman as a lady, but also as his equal. That's a tall order."

"Nah," Dakota said. "That's actually the easy part, especially if he has a taste for strong-willed, independent women, which I bet your son will because he has you as a role model."

She nearly choked on a sob that threatened to

escape her lips. No one since her parents died had described her with those types of adjectives. If anything, people saw her as weak and insecure.

Part of her knew that Dakota was building her up, because that's the kind of man he was, and she appreciated that.

But she also couldn't help but distrust his sweetness simply because she'd been taken for a ride by a man who once promised her the world with a cherry on top.

That said, she believed—no—she knew that Dakota wasn't Josh.

"That's sweet of you to say," Alabama said.

In the background, Hillary started to fuss.

"That's our cue to leave," Clayton said. "If we let her get to a full-fledged wail, she'll not only wake up the entire house, but she'll be up for the rest of the night."

"Yeah. It's best we go now when she still might actually fall asleep in the car." Sage stood. "And I need her to sleep all night because I still have the worst morning sickness in the world."

"I'll go warm up the car," Clayton said.

"I'll help." Dakota followed Clayton out the front door.

Alabama picked up the wine glasses along with the cheese and cracker tray while Sage prepared Hillary to go out into the cold Montana winter night. Alabama really enjoyed Sage and wanted to continue the friendship, but she still feared that one night soon, she'd be sneaking off into the night.

Or she'd end up dead at the hands of her husband.

It killed her that she was still legally married. If she never saw Josh again, it would be too soon.

"A penny for your thoughts," Sage said as she stood rocking back and forth in the family room by the fire with her daughter in her arms.

"Sorry. I'm just tired."

"It is getting late, but that's not it." Sage adjusted the blanket around Hillary before setting her on the sofa. "I don't want to frighten you, insult you, or upset you, but my husband and I run more than one shelter for battered women. I know the signs."

"And I know Dakota told you." While there was no reason to lie at this point, making a stand was something Alabama hadn't done since college. She clasped her hands behind her back and twisted at her fingers. "I know you're not a Brotherhood Protector employee like Dakota or your husband, but Dakota told me all about the work you do, and I think that's great. I'm honestly so appreciative of you and people like you who have made it possible for people like me to make a clean break and a fresh start. However, I don't want to talk about it, or bond over it. I'm sorry for being so rude, but after this moment, I don't want to ever have to discuss this again, unless I have to for the safety of my son, and no offense, I doubt that would be with you." Her lungs burned, and her knees shook. It had been years since she'd ever dared to be so bold. If she'd ever spoken to Josh like that, she would have been punished.

Had she spoken to the help like that when Josh didn't think it was called for, Alabama would have paid the price with a beating. And if she'd gone soft on anyone in service when Josh thought otherwise, again, she'd end up with bruises on her body.

Sage smiled. "The only thing I have to say to that is if it ever comes to an issue of safety, I sincerely hope you will feel comfortable talking to me. Otherwise, I look forward to playdates with our kids, and like I said, I'm not the best cook, but I'm happy to share the few things I know." She bent down and scooped up her daughter. "A bunch of us wives get together for Wine Wednesday. Consider yourself invited."

"I'm not a wife."

"That is true. But you're a nanny and a mom, and you work for a man who works for Hank. You will need wine on Wednesdays. I won't take no for an answer."

Before Alabama could respond, Sage had turned and headed out the door.

"I'M REALLY TORN." Dakota zipped up his fleece and tossed a stick for Buster to chase. "But if I put eyes on her husband, I could be asking for trouble I don't want and she doesn't need."

"And if you don't, you won't see him coming." Clayton slammed the vehicle door and stuffed his hands into his pockets. The headlights cut through the dark Montana night. Big puffy snowflakes floated in the sky, dancing in the moonlight.

When Dakota had first moved his family to Montana, he'd hated it, but his wife and the girls took to the land like Buster did to peanut butter hidden in a plastic toy. Now, he couldn't imagine living anywhere else.

"How high-profile is he?" Clayton asked.

"That's not even half of the problem." There were very few men or women in the Brotherhood Protectors that Dakota didn't trust one hundred percent, and that was only because he didn't know everyone or hadn't worked with all agents. But him and Clayton had a special bond and were more than brothers-in-arms. He knew Clayton wouldn't tell a single soul who Alabama's husband was, but that wasn't the point.

And Clayton didn't need to know.

Yet.

Clayton lowered his chin and arched a brow. "High-profile and dangerous to society. Sounds like my biological father."

"You're not that far off," Dakota said as he continued to toss the stick as far as he could so

Buster would tire himself out. He'd been much better around Alabama, but she still shied away from him, and Dakota wanted to change that. He wanted to change a lot of things about how Alabama reacted to the world around her, but he knew only time and distance from her old life would give her the freedom to find her confidence again. "And we do have a slight connection that I can use that wouldn't cause a red flag."

"Then use it."

"I've already spoken to Hank about it, and he's on board," Dakota said.

"Does he know who she is?"

Dakota shook his head. "He didn't want to know. He figured for now, it's best I'm the only one. If I see movement or any cause for concern, then I can blow the whistle, and we can act on her behalf, but until then, life goes on as normal."

"Only she hasn't found any kind of real normal yet, and that could take years." Clayton ran a hand over his head. His expression turned serious. "Do you have any idea how bad it was for her? What the beatings were like?"

"The only thing she's told me about it was that he beat her beyond recognition the night she gave birth and that Wyoming was born a month early because of it. I haven't asked any other questions specific to that. I figure if she wants to open up, she will, but I don't need the sordid details to have an idea of what her husband is capable of. I've seen what that asshole can do up-close and personal. He's bad news, and if he gets his hands on her, she's dead, and I don't even want to think about what he could do to that sweet little boy." He took the stick and snapped it in half on his thigh.

Buster yelped as he sat at Dakota's feet. "Sorry, buddy," Dakota said, letting out a long breath, doing his best to calm the rage boiling in his veins. "Thing is, I totally believe Chauncey sent her here for a reason, but he hasn't responded to my call, and that makes me even more nervous."

"Would you like me to reach out to him?" Clayton asked.

"I don't know. I'm worried that will red flag something in the underground."

"It shouldn't. My mom's foundation does a lot work with him and his shelter. I can drop hints he'll understand without coming out and asking. If he's not responding, it's for a reason, and we'll just have to trust him."

"I feel like I'm flying blind, and I don't like that, and this bullshit with Candice and the Hooker family, God only knows who Chad's father is aligning himself with. Did you know he's working with the Carpelli family? That's moving to big time mafia crap." Dakota had Trish, one of the IT geniuses, do some poking around into any connections the Hookers could have to certain high-profile crime families without giving her the Brolin name. So far, Josh and his family hadn't come into her searches.

But that didn't mean that the Hookers weren't on Josh's radar, especially since the Carpellis were connected to the Brolins through a distant family marriage and the running of a night club in Vegas.

"Hooker is small-time, and no one, including the Carpellis, take him seriously. He's just a drug runner, and the DEA has an eye on a few shipments coming through. Hooker is sloppy, and he's either going to get busted by the cops or killed by the Carpellis. The only thing you have to worry about is how that plays out with little Hooker and Candice."

"She moved out of her grandfather's house and in with Chad. That doesn't make me comfortable at all," Dakota said. "And I heard she and Chad both plan on moving to Vegas."

"If they do, then you've got nothing to worry about," Clayton said.

"Yeah, except I worry about Candice. She's immature, and she's making some really bad decisions."

"She's a grown-ass woman, and you're not her keeper." Clayton pointed to the house. "And, for the record, you're not hers either."

Dakota laughed. "That's funny coming from you."

Clayton raced around to the other side of the car and opened the back passenger door as his wife carried out their little girl. "I'm just suggesting you check your motives because you're falling fast and hard."

"Even funnier coming from you." Dakota choked on his breath. He didn't want to believe that he could have developed any real feelings for Alabama in such a short time. All he wanted was to make sure nothing bad happened. "And I'm just doing what anyone one of us would do for someone like Alabama and her son."

"You keep telling yourself that." Sage shut the door after buckling Hillary into the car seat. "And it is true. Anyone from the Brotherhood Protectors would help her, but they wouldn't necessarily move her into their home and make them their nanny. They also wouldn't find ways to constantly touch her, flirt with her, or act like a boyfriend on a double date."

"I didn't behave like that at all," Dakota protested. However, his mind wandered back to certain parts of the evening, and he absolutely treated the night as if he and Alabama were a couple and they were sharing their dinner with another couple. It had felt familiar, yet different in a weird way to do that.

And not once had he felt as though he was being disrespectful of his late wife, something that always happened when he'd actually found himself remotely interested in a woman.

Sage stood inches from him and cupped his face with her warm hands. "Personally, I think it's wonderful. She seems like a really great person. But there is something none of us want to say out loud, and it's worse than her husband showing up and beating her again."

Dakota pinched the bridge of his nose. It's not like he hadn't thought about this and lost sleep over it, especially now that he knew the identity of her husband. "Kidnapping charges and it might not matter that her husband is a wife beater."

CHAPTER 7

"COME ON, little man, you can do it." Dakota sat on the floor with his arms stretched wide while Wyoming held on to the coffee table with a big smile.

Wyoming lifted his hand and waved.

"Come here. You can do it. I know you can. Walk to me so we can show Mama when she gets out of the shower."

"Mama is right here." Alabama sat on the floor next to Dakota, smelling of a strawberry patch. "Where are the girls?"

"Upstairs brushing their teeth. I told them they could come down and say good night, but then right to bed. It's already an hour past their bedtime."

"I'm surprised that little guy isn't passed out cold."

Dakota wiggled his fingers.

Alabama did the same. "Come to Mama."

"Ma Ma," Wyoming said with a squeal of delight as he let go of the coffee table and took a single step.

"That's it. You can do it." Wyoming continued to wobble across the family room floor, one chubby leg at a time.

He laughed with each step as if he knew what he was doing would cause everyone such joy.

"Daddy, he's walking!" River skidded to a stop, landing in her father's lap just as Wyoming fell forward into Dakota's lap as well.

"Traitor," Alabama said with a chuckle.

"Da da," Wyoming explained, resting his head on Dakota's shoulder and curling his fingers around his neck.

Dakota closed his eyes tight for a brief moment before blinking them open. "It's Dakota." He patted the toddler on the back.

Alabama stared at him with a single tear dribbling down her cheek.

He reached out and wiped it away. "It's just because he hears my girls call me dad. And Dakota starts with Da. We can just keep correcting him, and he'll figure it out." Only the sentiment filled his soul. He wanted Alabama and her son in his life in the forever kind of way, or at least, he wanted to see what that might feel like. See how his girls took to him dating, for real.

Sage and Clayton were right on target, because

the idea of Alabama walking out of his world made his heart physically hurt.

He continued to stare into Alabama's sweet eyes. Her lashes blinked wildly, but she didn't say a single word.

"Daddy," Sky said, standing by the staircase. "I'm ready for bed."

"Think you two girls can handle taking Wyoming, changing his diaper, and getting him in his crib? If he fusses, just sing to him, or read him a book, but otherwise, give him his blanket and see if he'll just lay down and go to sleep."

"Dad, we've put him to bed before." Sky lifted Wyoming into her arms and headed down the hallway with River skipping behind her.

Dakota helped Alabama to the sofa. He had no idea what to say or how to respond. "That boy is going to be running soon."

She nodded.

"He doesn't know what Da Da really means."

"But he does. He knows it means you to the girls. He hugged you after he said it like he hugs me after he calls me mom."

"I'll give you that, but he doesn't really understand the gravity of it." He took her hands into his and ran his thumb over her silky skin. In the couple of weeks she'd been living in the house and taking care of his girls, they'd become close friends. He cared about her in ways he never thought he would be able to after

Lunar died. "But you do know I care for him a great deal."

"I think that's why it stunned me. While he's never really been a shy baby, he's never been this attached to people. He actually got fussy when you left for work this morning."

"Maybe he's coming down with something."

She tilted her head. "When I leave the house, even if it's just to get something from the car, he freaks out, so for him to fuss over you, that's attachment. The underground told me to never get too comfortable because staying in one place too long could be a deadly mistake."

"Not in your case." He sucked in a deep breath and let it out slowly. "Over the last couple of weeks, I've been thinking a lot about your specific situation and what Chauncey told Clayton."

"They spoke? When? Why didn't you tell me?"

"Because I just found out today," he said, tucking a piece of her hair behind her ear. "It was all pretty cryptic, but the basic message was that he believes your identity was compromised somewhere, and the concern is more about Josh taking Wyoming from you. The last reports we've seen on the hunt for you is that Josh is only concerned for your mental stability and the safety of his son. You are wanted for kidnapping and unfortunately, the way the system—"

She bolted upright. "I know all too well how the fucking system works. I get I'm a fugitive, and I know they will take him if I'm caught, which is why I can't stay in one place. I can't ever let him get his hands on Wyoming. He'll turn him into a criminal."

"I'm not going to let that happen." Slowly, he closed the gap, taking her into his arms. "I don't just care about Wyoming. I care about you." He cupped her cheeks and gave her slow, sweet kiss. He kept it controlled and tender. He wanted to show her how much he valued her and respected her.

"I wish you didn't," she whispered. "I wish I didn't."

He chuckled. "I'm not sure how to take that."

She rested her hands on his shoulders. "It's crazy for us to even think about being together."

"What's crazy is for us not to think about it." He kissed her nose. "And crazier for us not to discuss how to ensure your safety, forever. Which means, putting Josh in jail."

She gasped. "He's untouchable."

"No one is that protected." He pressed his finger on her lips. "It's time for me to sit down with my boss and tell him everything."

"Why would you do that?"

"So I can take him down, prove what he did to you, and all the other criminal things he's into. That way you and Wyoming can stop looking over your shoulders and have a quiet, relatively normal life, hopefully here with me and my girls."

She shook her head like a rabid dog. "No. No. I can't be anywhere near him. I can't go back."

"Alabama. I'm not asking you to. You don't even have to go back to using your birth name. My team will do all the heavy lifting. Josh won't know you had anything to do with it. He'll never know where you are or who you are even when we put that bastard behind bars."

"What if it doesn't work?" she asked with wide eyes. "It didn't work for Leslie."

"We're going to take a very different approach. We won't take chances, and I'm sure as hell not handing anything over to the FBI with some weak-ass case. I'm sorry about what happened with your friend. I wish I could go back and do things differently. I could say things like I was led, or we didn't know about—"

"I don't blame you for Leslie," she said with a slight tremble in her voice. "But I'm scared. I feel like no matter what I do, I'm taking a risk with my life and my son's."

He cupped her face. "You are. But I, Hank, and the rest of the Brotherhood Protectors can develop a plan that is less risky and gives you a really good chance at a future free from worrying if Josh is going to find you and hurt you. Please, let me do this."

"If I said no and I wanted to leave, you'd let me?"

"I'd beg and plead with you, but at the end of the day, yes. I would."

She leaned closer, tilting her head. "I can't explain why I trust you so much. Deep down, I know not all men who show kindness when I first meet them end up as wife beaters. I know you're one of the good guys. I can feel it, but I can't even trust myself."

"It's up to me to show you what kind of man I am by the way I treat you. Give it and me some time."

Her smile grew wider. "I plan on it. I'm giving you my blessing to do whatever you need to in order to make sure I'm not going to get arrested and my son will never have to be around Josh. I don't ever want him to know that man is biologically related to him at all, and I don't want to sneak out of your window and disappear into the night. I just want my second chance to do it right this time." Her plump lips pressed against his in a soft, but passionate kiss. Their tongues tangled and twisted in a promise of something wild and wicked, while being romantic and sweet all at the same time.

Giggles from the hallway caught his attention, and he broke off the kiss. "We have little eyes watching us."

"So I heard," she whispered.

"I better go tuck them in. Will you have a glass of wine with me after?"

"I'd like that," she said.

"I like you."

∿

ALABAMA QUICKLY CHECKED on her sleeping child before racing to the bathroom to freshen her makeup and put on a little body spray.

Leaning against the sink, she stared at herself in the mirror. A year ago, her eyes were swollen shut. Her lips were cracked open. She had bruises and cuts all over her body.

A year ago, she thought for sure she was going to die and so was her son.

For the last eleven months, she'd been traveling from one place to the next not really living and barely surviving. The only thing that held her together had been Wyoming.

And now she found herself in the midst of the kind of family life she remembered having as a kid and the kind of family she'd wanted for herself.

It all seemed too good to be true.

"Are you okay?" Dakota asked.

She jumped. "Shit. You scared me."

"Sorry, but when you didn't come back out or answer when I called you, I thought I should check things out."

"It's okay. But if I'm being honest, I'm all over the map right now."

He slipped his fingers through hers and tugged her into the main room of the apartment. "I left the door open so I can hear the girls if they need me," he said as he sat down on the sofa.

She made herself comfortable, tucking her feet

under her butt and leaning against his strong fore-arm. She stifled a yawn. "Want to hear something funny?"

"Sure."

"My parents were pretty well off. Actually, they were rich. I was a spoiled kid, never having to think about money, but my parents did make me work, and they taught me the value of a dollar. When I went to college, I had every intention of getting off my parents' money train. When they died, I was so clue-less about what to do and how to handle things, and Josh was just so willing to help. I thought he was my knight in shining armor, and sometimes, I look at you and I think, if he's too good to be true, run and run fast."

"I have flaws and lots of them, but one thing you can count on is that I will never hit you or hurt you physically, but I don't understand what's funny about any of this."

"A few things are, actually. The first one being my rich-ass husband has all my parents' money now."

"That's really not funny."

"It is when I think about how desperate I was in college to learn how to take care of myself and how quickly I ended up letting someone else take care of me, and now I'm doing it again."

"That's where you're wrong, because I'm not taking care of you. I'm helping you solve a problem."

She glanced down at their hands. His seemed so

127

massive over hers, and his calloused skin grazed hers, sending a warm shiver over her body.

"You've taken me in, given me a place to live."

He pressed his finger over her lips. "You pay me rent, and yes, I gave you a job, but I needed to find a nanny quickly. Whether that be a temporary situation or not, that was up to you."

"That brings me to what I think is really funny, and that's the fact I got my degree in early childhood education. Of the jobs I was applying for, this is really the only one I'm truly qualified to do, though during the school year, your kids are gone more than they are home." She tossed her head back and laughed. "I thought if I were a schoolteacher, I'd really know what it was like to live like the rest of the world. I've been so clueless my entire life."

"Not clueless," he whispered, pressing his lips on her cheek. "You might have had blinders on for a while, but most of us do in our youth."

"You really are too good to be true."

"I've never mastered making the bed, putting down the toilet seat, and I have a tendency to take charge without asking other people if that's what they want."

"Only the last one is truly a shortcoming."

"I'm sure as you get to know me better, you'll find many more." He kissed her neck just under her earlobe. "I haven't wanted to be with a woman in a long time."

Her heart pounded in her ears as she wondered if she heard him correctly. She couldn't imagine he'd ever go very long without a girlfriend. He was the kind of man every woman wanted to bring home.

"Why not?" she asked with a shaky voice.

He leaned back and stared at her with laden eyes. "At first, I was too grief-stricken to even think about it. Then, after a while, as I navigated my way into being a single father, I was focused solely on my girls. Recently, when I've thought that I might like to have someone to share my life again, I look around, and I think there isn't anyone I'd want to introduce into my children's life that way until you and Wyoming drive onto my ranch, and now I find myself jumping in with both feet, and each time I tell myself to slow down, I speed up."

She held his gaze, her pulse raging out of control. She hadn't felt like a desirable woman since she'd met Josh. He'd taken all that away from her, and now, in a flash, Dakota has her insides twisted and begging for affection that only a true gentleman could give. "I don't know if I can do this." The shame of all the things Josh did came down on her like a tidal wave. Fear grabbed ahold of her heart, and it wouldn't let go.

Memories bombarded her mind. There had been so much she tried to block out.

"Hey," he said, cupping her cheeks. "Stay here with me; don't go back there."

"Sorry," she whispered. 'It's just...just..."

"I know what he did. You don't have to say."

"I think I do." She stiffened her spine, forcing herself to sit tall and proud. She needed to pull herself together. She needed to remind herself that she wasn't the sum of what Josh did, but who she chose to be, and she chose not to be a victim anymore. But in order for her to move past everything that had happened, she needed to acknowledge everything.

He drew a hand over his face before leaning forward and snagging one of the glasses of wine. "I might need to be drunk to hear this; otherwise, I might want to go put my fist through a wall."

"Why? It didn't happen to you."

"It shouldn't happen to anyone," he said with venom laced in his words. "It angers me that it happened to someone I've come to care about, again."

"Again?" she asked as she swallowed her breath.

"I had a close friend in high school who was repeatedly raped by her boyfriend. It was hard for me because I didn't see it, or maybe I turned a blind eye to it because he was on the lacrosse team with me. I don't know, but no one found out until she ended up in the hospital. She never really recovered or got the help she needed. I heard she committed suicide a few years ago."

"That's horrible. I'm so sorry." Alabama often prayed for death during beatings or when her husband raped her, but she also learned to close her mind to what was happening to her, almost as if she were having an out-of-body experience, only the aftermath made her a walking zombie. While she knew how to play the part Josh wanted her to play and be the pretty wife on his arm, and she did all the things he wanted, she did so without any emotional connect to anyone or anything. "The hardest part about being in an abusive relationship for me has been the ability to look back and see all the signs, and yet I didn't even realize it until the first time he'd left visible bruises on my body and I had to stay inside in fear of what people would think of me, not him. And when it turned into rape, I kept telling myself he was my husband, and this was what married couples did. That he had a right to my body."

Dakota closed his eyes and took in a sharp breath. "I really hate that this happened to you." He blinked.

She rested her hand on his chest, feeling it rise and fall with each deep breath. If she wasn't mistaken, his eyes glossed over.

"I do too. It's hard to break that internal dialogue that says if only I had done things his way, he wouldn't have had to hit me. If only I hadn't said no, he wouldn't have had to force me."

Dakota opened his mouth, but she shushed him.

"I hear what I'm saying, and I know it's absurd and crazy and not true, but—"

He curled his fingers around her wrist and tugged

her hand away. "That's not what I was going to say because you don't need me to tell you that."

"What were you going to say then?"

"In the month that you've lived between my tiny house and the apartment, you've changed. A lot. You're stronger. More confident. When you first moved in, you couldn't even look me in the eye for more than thirty seconds. You were timid and afraid of your own shadow. Now, you're driving around town in my SUV, making friends, doing normal everyday things that last year you wouldn't have ever considered doing. You're breaking that dialogue. You're becoming the woman you want to be, and no one, including me, is going to stand in your way. I just hope I can be part of your life and uplift you in all the ways you deserve."

"You make it impossible to push you away."

He brought her hand to his lips. "Maybe we should call it a night. Besides, tomorrow is your birthday and Valentine's Day. I have a few special things planned. Well, the girls do. They really want to make it memorable."

"Two weeks ago, I would have skipped out of any kind of celebration. But not now." Boldly, she leaned in and gave him a passionate goodnight kiss. It was meant to end the evening on a positive note. It wasn't meant to last more than a minute or two. Just a quick swirl of the tongue. She wanted to let him know that she was doing her best to be open to the possibility of dating and potentially a future that could include them being together long term.

It was a crazy thought, but wasn't running from her husband all about starting over? Making a new life for her and Wyoming?

Every nerve ending in her body ignited. She straddled his lap and dug her fingers into his thick shoulder muscles. She couldn't remember the last time she felt this feminine.

This sexy.

Or this alive.

She pulled at the fabric of his shirt, desperate to feel the heat of skin. For the last year, everyone in the underground would ask her if she could do anything, be anyone, what would that look like, and she couldn't answer.

Now she had an idea.

Abruptly, she broke off the kiss. "Are there preschools around here that might be looking for teachers that might let me bring a kid to work? That wouldn't interfere with the work I do for you at all."

"Interesting conversation to start while you're sitting on me." He gripped her hips and pulled her closer. "But to answer your question, yes, there are. And I think that's a great idea for you. We can discuss it and work on your resume tomorrow, but for now, I either need to say good night, or take you to bed. I'm good with either, though I do have a preference."

It amazed her how comfortable she felt with

Dakota and how his comment made her insides go wild with desire. "I can feel your preference."

His cheeks turned red. "I wish I could control that physical reaction, but I can't. However, I can stand up and walk out that door."

"I'm sure you can, and I still might make you, but for now, I don't want you to," she said, losing some of her newfound confidence. "I don't want to be a tease and lead you on."

"Stop," he said. "We can kiss, snuggle, touch, do nothing, sleep, whatever. I just want to know that I have a chance with you."

She swallowed.

Hard.

Lifting her shirt over her head, she tossed it to the floor. "I need you to know that this second, right now, I'm all in. That might change."

"Shhhh." He kissed her lips. Her cheeks. Her neck. He pressed his palm under the swell of her breast. "I want to pick you up and take you to bed. I want to make mad passionate love to you all night. I want to hold you afterward and whisper how wonderful you are in your ear. But that's not what I need. What I need is for you to feel safe in my arms, and I will do whatever it takes for you to feel that way."

"Take me to bed," she said.

CHAPTER 8

TAKE ME TO BED.

The words echoed in Dakota's brain as he gently lay Alabama down on the queen mattress in the apartment. Careful not to put all his weight on her, he shifted to the side, but still settling between her legs, his lips locked with hers in a decadent kiss. He wanted to be wild and free, but he also wanted to treat her with the kind of respect she deserved.

He needed to let her control the situation, and that would prove to be difficult. Not because he couldn't let a woman rule him in bed. Of course he could. But he wanted to ravish her body and bring her pleasure like she'd never experienced before.

He believed he could do that, but it would have to wait.

Tonight would be about her taking back her sexuality.

Tonight he would give her whatever she wanted, and if that meant he had to stop right in the middle of the throws of passion, then so be it. He'd deal with it because he cared.

More than he should.

More than he wanted to.

But he knew she was worth risking his heart over.

"Alabama?"

"Yes?"

"Promise me you will communicate with me, and if anything makes you feel uncomfortable, you'll tell me." He lifted her into his arms and made his way toward the apartment bedroom. "And please understand I can't stay the entire night. My girls are at an age where they understand more than I want them to."

"I don't want them to wake up and find you in my room," she murmured against his ear. "I don't want to ever come between you and your girls."

"Wrong circumstance to say this and not the perfect time, but if you were ever to pose a problem between me and my girls, we wouldn't happen. I'm sorry, but they are my number one priority."

"Don't be sorry, but could you stop talking and start kissing and touching?" She rested her hand high on his thighs.

"I think I can handle that," he murmured. He focused his attention on removing the rest of her clothing, as well as his all the while kissing every curve of her body. He didn't let any inch of her go unnoticed. He made sure both breasts were fully appreciated. He suckled both nipples as though each one were the only reason he lived. He kissed her skin from her temples to the edge of her big toe. He did everything he could think of to drive her crazy and show her he cared more about her pleasure than his own.

He captured her soft moans in his mouth as he dipped his fingers slowly inside. Her hips raised up and rolled with each stroke. Her fingers dug into his shoulders, and she tossed her head back, biting down on her lower lip.

His breath hitched. Watching her arousal grow and intensify at his touch humbled and excited him.

The faster she rolled her hips, the more the desire to taste her became unbearable. He kissed his way down to her belly button. "Do you like this?" he asked, lowering his head.

"Oh, yes," she said between ragged breaths. "Very much."

"Good, because so do I." He switched between his tongue and fingers, bringing her close to climax, teasing her, and testing his own control, which would snap the second he entered her if he wasn't careful.

Her grip on his head tightened, and she clasped her legs tight. Her stomach trembled, and his name rolled off her tongue like melting butter.

With each tender flick of his tongue, her body rewarded him with another shudder until her muscles contracted one last time, and she relaxed under him, taking in a long breath.

He lay next to her, running his fingers up and down her arm and kissing her shoulder. "How do you feel?"

She turned her head and smiled. "You really need a verbal answer after that?"

He chuckled. "I suppose not."

"And now it's my turn." She pushed him to his back and pressed her plump lips against his chest.

His skin sizzled against her touch. Her fingers were warm and curled around him with just the right pressure to render him speechless. No matter how hard he tried, he couldn't fill his lungs with enough air. They burned as if someone took a blowtorch to them. The room spun, and everything blurred but her pretty lips on his body.

"Alabama," he managed to croak out. "You don't have to do this." He gripped the sheets, staring down at her, not wanting to touch her in fear he'd run his hands through her hair, tugging or pushing, and that might make her feel cornered, or trapped.

Or worse, forced.

He couldn't have that.

With a dainty finger she tucked a piece of hair behind her ear and smiled. "I want to. Don't you like it?"

He arched a brow. "Oh, I like it. Actually, I love it. But I don't want you to feel like you have to do it because you think I want it or something."

"Do you want it?" She held him in her hand, gently stroking, rolling her thumb over the tip.

"Yeah."

"Then just enjoy it."

He watched as she took him into her hot mouth, her hands exploring while her tongue did things to him he hadn't ever experienced. Digging his heels into the bed, he squeezed his eyes shut and tried to enjoy the moment while focusing on everything but the woman currently giving him the greatest pleasure in the world.

That only lasted a couple of minutes.

He blinked his eyes open and damn near lost it when he glanced down at the blond hair pooling over his stomach. "Okay, that's enough." He gave her a quick, but gentle tug. "Come here."

He had every intention of kissing her good and hard while flipping her on her back, but she had a different plan.

"Oh, dear, God. You're going to be the death of me," he ground out as she straddled him, taking him slowly inside, inch by inch.

Her hips rolled back and forth over him. She pressed her hands against his chest, and her hair tickled his skin.

Twisting and tugging at her nipples, he focused

on her body, and not his. He desperately wanted her to orgasm one more time before he lost all control. It scared him how much she mattered to him in such a short time, but at the same time, he hadn't felt this alive in a long time.

"Oh, God," she said with a throaty moan. She dug into his chest with her nails and rode him faster and harder.

He curled his toes, holding her hips as her body shuddered over his, sending hot searing messages to his brain. He could no longer contain his resolve. He raised his hips, thrusting inside her rapidly a few times as he exploded. "Alabama," he murmured, pulling her to his lips and kissing her as hard as they made love, matching their movements until she fell over his body spent and exhausted.

Carefully, he covered them with the sheets and held her close. He kissed her temple and stroked her hair. Tenderly, he rubbed her arm and shoulder. He stared at the ceiling, knowing he should get up and go to his own bed.

But he didn't want to move.

Just a couple more minutes.

"Dakota?"

"Yes," he said.

"What did you tell the girls about us kissing?"

He smiled. "They asked me if they could rip up the potential dating list."

"And what did you say?"

140

"I told them that I only dated one lady at a time and that if you'd let me date you, then they could burn that stupid list."

Alabama snuggled in closer. "Just please, don't be too good to be true."

"I'm not perfect. I'm sure I will say and do some dumb things that will make you mad at me. I'm not some superhero or knight in shining armor. I'm just a man." He took her chin with his thumb and forefinger and tilted her head, forcing her to look him in the eye. "Don't put me on a pedestal, because I will let you down if you do that, and that would really upset me."

WAKING up alone had been both a relief and a source of fear. She hadn't expected to fall asleep in Dakota's arms last night. And she did expect, when he left, for him to say goodbye.

But that didn't happen.

She lifted the sheets and groaned. When she'd been living with Josh, she couldn't stand to sleep naked all night in fear of what he'd do, and also, she just didn't feel comfortable in her own skin.

Last night she not only lost herself completely with Dakota, but she gained a piece of her womanhood back. He might be just a man, but he was a special man, and any woman who ended up with him was one lucky lady.

She giggled as she put on her sweatpants and nightshirt. After last night, she had to consider herself to be the lucky one. Her heart fluttered. The fear of her past crept into her mind and soul. None of them could be considered lucky if Josh came into their lives, and if anything ever happened to Dakota or his girls, that would be Alabama's fault.

She couldn't live with that.

Quickly, she checked on Wyoming. Still sound asleep.

She peeked her head out the door, in search of the dog. In the few weeks she'd lived in the house, she'd still not gotten used to the damn dog, but Buster certainly had become accustomed to her living there. "Oh, for Pete's sake. Why do you have to sit by my door every morning?"

The dog thumped his tail and whined.

"Buster, get back here," Dakota whispered.

Stupid dog jumped to his feet but didn't race off toward his master. Instead, he nudged the door with his snout.

"Wyoming is still sleeping, now scoot."

"I'm sorry," Dakota said as he padded down the hallway wearing nothing but flannel pajama bottoms and a white V-neck undershirt that fit tight across his firm chest.

A moan got caught in her throat, remembering his naked, tight body. Heat raced to her cheeks.

"My dog seems to like you more than me," he said with a wink and a smile.

"I wish that weren't true." She sidestepped both dog and owner, making a beeline for the kitchen and a fresh pot of coffee. The one thing the apartment didn't have was a working stovetop and oven, something Dakota promised to have fixed within the month. But until then, she was given free rein of his kitchen, which made sense because during the school week, she needed to feed the girls breakfast and dinner. "But at least I know he's not going to eat me."

Dakota laughed. "Hey," he said, curling his fingers around her forearm and turning her to face him. "Happy birthday."

She let out a long breath. "I was hoping you'd forget." Her stomach growled when she inhaled a mixture of bitter coffee and sweet cinnamon.

"No way." He tilted his head, looking down the hall. "All clear." He leaned in and brushed his lips across hers. It caught her off guard, and she had to fist his shirt in order to keep herself from falling over. "Mind going back to bed? The girls are making you breakfast."

"I told you I didn't want a fuss."

"It's just breakfast. And well, a romantic dinner tonight with just the two of us because it is Valentine's Day."

She opened her mouth in protest, but he shushed her with his finger.

"We'll talk about that later. For now, the girls are about done with the feast," he said.

"I'm doing this for them, not you." She poked him in the chest. The last thing she wanted to do was disappoint Sky and River. "And tonight isn't going to happen. We don't have a babysitter."

He laughed. "We won't be needing one, but we'll discuss that later."

"Ma Ma," Wyoming wailed.

Dakota gave her a little shove toward the apartment. "You get back in bed, and I'll go give the little man some cereal."

"I'm only doing this for the girls." She cocked her head and glared, giving him her best *I'm not thrilled but I'm taking one for the team* look. "Otherwise, I'd be taking my coffee and going to my room to spend my day off alone."

He cupped her chin.

Her breath hitched.

"Only a half day. Don't forget I have to go into the office this morning."

She groaned. "To talk about me?"

He chuckled. "Hank and I will have a conversation, but I'm on research duty for a case Maddog is working, and he needs me to do some things."

"Go ahead and work all day, if you need to. No need to do anything for me tonight."

"If you really want to be alone, then I'll cancel the

plans, but that will make me sad." He scooted past her and scooped Wyoming up into his arms.

"Dada," Wyoming said.

"Da-ko-ta." Dakota batted Wyoming's nose.

"Dada." Wyoming buried his head in Dakota's neck.

"You." Dakota pointed to the bed. "Get back in that. The girls will be back with your feast shortly."

She kissed her son and then climbed into the bed and snagged her Kindle off the nightstand. She pulled up the mystery novel she'd downloaded earlier in the week. Her goal had been to finish it today, if Wyoming would let her.

"Good morning!" Sky carefully entered her room carrying a tray of eggs, bacon, pancakes, and fresh coffee. "Happy birthday and happy Valentine's Day!"

"Why, thank you," she said as sweetly as possible. "I hope you got my cards and chocolate that I left out for you last night."

"We did, but Daddy said we can't have it until after lunch," Sky said with a pouty face.

"Probably a good idea." Alabama placed the tray over her lap and raised the mug to her lips and took a sip. "Your father makes the best coffee."

"He makes the best pancakes too," Sky said. "But I made the eggs and bacon."

"And I picked out your gift," River said as she skipped into the room. The child didn't walk anywhere. Her energy and enthusiasm were intoxicating and contagious. She plopped herself on the bed holding out three wrapped gifts. "This one is from me and Sky. That one is from Daddy. And that one is from Wyoming." River leaned in. "I picked that one out too. But Daddy's present is the best. I'd save it for last."

"River. You're supposed to wait for Dad to finish feeding Wyoming. Besides, if she opens the gifts now, her food will get cold."

Alabama blinked back the tears that threatened to flow like a raging waterfall. When she first drove onto this ranch, she never in million years would have thought she'd become part of a family. She'd planned on living out her life, just her and her son, without having any close personal friends. She couldn't afford to risk it.

Only, she'd already given her heart.

And her son's as well.

She dived into her breakfast, focusing on all the flavors and not the emotions swirling around in her soul.

"This little guy doesn't want to miss out on the fun," Dakota said as he strolled into the bedroom. He set Wyoming on the bed before he removed the tray and joined everyone else...on the bed.

Buster whined at the foot, but thankfully, didn't jump up.

"It's present time," River said, holding out one. "Start with Wyoming's."

"All right." With shaky fingers, she ripped off the paper and pulled out a bracelet that had two heart pieces. One with her name and one with her son's name. "Oh. This is so beautiful. Thank you."

"Thank Wyoming. It's from him," River said with a proud smile, holding out a second gift. "This is from me and Sky. Open it."

"Give her a second to breathe," Sky said.

Alabama's heart beat out of control. She couldn't believe they went to all this trouble. "Oh my. This is beautiful." She swiped at her cheeks, hoping no one saw the tears rolling from her eyes. Back in the day, she had a fetish for all things designer handbags. She wouldn't think twice about dropping a couple thousand dollars on a single bag. Now, anything over twenty bucks was out of her budget, and why would she need more than one?

"We saw you looking at that purse when we were in town," Sky said. "So we called Daddy, and he picked it up for us, but we paid for it with our own money."

"That is so sweet. You two girls didn't need to do that for me." Alabama remembered admiring the bag and being shocked it was only twenty dollars.

"But we wanted to," River said.

Alabama held out her arms and hugged both girls. Of course, Wyoming had to get in on the action.

"Okay, little man." Dakota lifted him off the pile of girls. "Time for your mama to open my present.

Dakota rested Wyoming on his lap while his girls handed her the last gift. "Now, this isn't just for you. It's for Wyoming as well."

"Da Ka. Da Da." Wyoming cupped Dakota's cheeks and gave him a big kiss.

Watching her son with Dakota and the way their bond grew stronger and stronger each day created a tug of war inside Alabama's soul. She knew deep down how good it would be for Wyoming to have a father figure in his life, especially with a man like Dakota.

But he wasn't his father, and she still didn't know if she could or would stay.

"Sounds like he already knows what it is," she said.

"He does," Dakota said with a slight chuckle. "And for the record, this wasn't just my idea. The girls also agreed, but we thought it might help with your fear."

"My fear of what?" She held the gift in her lap and stared at Dakota. "Because the only thing I'm scared of right now is you and what you might have gotten me."

"Girls, go get the box. Uncle Maddog left it in the garage early this morning."

"It's here?" River jumped off the bed and twirled around. "Why didn't you tell us?"

"Just go get it," he said, taking the box from Alabama. "This is really just for show. All that's in here is a picture of what I got you."

Buster started barking and running in circles at the end of the bed.

"Sit down and relax," Dakota commanded.

Buster didn't listen.

"Sit. Now," Alabama said.

Buster did as commanded.

"That's impressive." Dakota shook his head. "You're a little traitor dog." He waggled a finger at Buster.

"I'm just glad he listens to me," she said. "The other day he was running at me so fast I thought if he didn't stop, he'd knock me over."

"He's gotten better as he's gotten older," he said. "We got him when Sky was little. She was terrified of dogs, and we thought this was the best way to help her overcome her fears. And it worked."

The sound of tiny yelping caught her attention. She whipped her head around. "Oh. No. You didn't get me a puppy. What the hell am I going to do with a puppy?" She smacked her hands against her cheeks.

The girls set a box down on her bed, and this cute chubby black bundle of fur sat and glanced up at her with floppy ears and a cocked head. Its little tail swished back and forth against the cardboard.

"His name is Apollo," Sky said. "He's a German shepherd. They are good, loyal dogs who are pretty mellow. Maddog had a whole litter of them. He said this is the best one."

"The best part is he's basically housebroken,"

Dakota said. "But I can help train him, and there is a good training class we can sign you up for."

Alabama glanced between the puppy glaring at her and Dakota. "You got me a dog? What am I supposed to do with a dog?" There were a lot of possible gift ideas that went through her mind that he could have gotten her, but a pet hadn't been one of them. As a kid, she'd always wanted a pet, but dogs terrified her, and her parents didn't like cats, so she had a goldfish.

When it died, she decided pets weren't her thing. The older she got, the more spoiled she became, and the idea of being around dirty animals made her cringe.

Looking at Apollo and Buster, she realized animals weren't necessarily dirty, but she was too closed-minded and too much of a snob to be bothered. She reached into the box and patted the puppy on the head twice before snatching her hand back when he tried to lick it.

"Girls, why don't you take Wyoming into the main family room and you can watch a cartoon for a bit."

"Daddy, we want to play with Apollo," River protested.

"There will be plenty of time for that," he said.

Ignoring the puppy's sharp fang-like teeth, she lifted Apollo out of the box and set him on her lap.

He got all excited and wiggly and kept trying to climb up her chest to lick her face.

"He likes you," Sky said as she lifted Wyoming into her arms. "Come on, buddy. Let's go find something fun to watch."

Alabama stared at Apollo, who stared back at her with the same curious expression that she figured she sported.

"You have to admit he's adorable," Dakota said.

"Yeah. But I know this kind of dog. They grow to be big and vicious."

"They can be." Dakota pushed himself to the head of the bed. He stretched out his legs, crossing his ankles. "They make for good watch dogs for their owners. Buster makes a lot of noise when people come to the house, but all he'd ever do is lick you to death. Not that you want a dog that would ever hurt anyone, but having one that would protect you, well, that might give you some peace of mind."

"You got me a dog to watch over me?"

"If you ever decide to leave me and the girls, I'd want you to have your own warning system, so to speak," Dakota said. "And this will help you overcome your fear of dogs in general."

A guttural sob caught in her throat. She covered her mouth. No one in her adult life had ever done anything so kind and thoughtful. Most people she'd known while being married to Josh cared only about their padded bank accounts and whether or not they had the newest, latest and greatest gadget and the most expensive car on the block.

"You don't have to keep him if you don't want to. Maddog has a long list of potential owners."

"No. No." She lifted Apollo and brought the puppy to her shoulder, giving it a big hug. "I want him. Thank you." She set the puppy back in the box. "If you don't want me to put you on a pedestal, you need to stop doing things that make you out to be Mr. Wonderful."

"I'll work on it."

CHAPTER 9

DAKOTA CHECKED THE TIME. He'd promised Alabama and his girls he'd be home by three. He didn't often work on weekends, but Maddog's case had taken a weird turn and he needed help, which Dakota was happy to do.

When Dakota first came to the Brotherhood Protectors, Hank had made it easy for him to work, take care of his kids, and help his wife battle cancer. Even when it became apparent that his wife wasn't going to win, Hank made sure Dakota had everything he needed, and that included work when he wanted.

After Lunar died, Hank, and everyone else in the Brotherhood, was there to help him pick up the pieces.

Nothing had changed, and Dakota would do anything for any member of the team. This was the family he chose.

His work cell buzzed, flashing a private number. That usually wasn't a good sign.

"Dakota here," he said.

"It's Chauncey. We're secure?"

"I'm at the office surrounded by empty desks waiting for Hank to discuss my situation, so, yup."

"You could have just said yes," Chauncey replied with a short laugh. "Sorry I've been MIA and what little communication I've had hasn't been direct. I'm being overly cautious."

"I appreciate that," Dakota said. "Do you have a straightforward answer for me?"

"I didn't know who she was until the night before her scheduled departure. You know me. I don't want to know who I'm dealing with, but I saw something on television regarding the case, and then I remembered a conversation I had with a person before she arrived, and it made me wonder who else might have figured out who she really was. That's why I sent her to you."

"So, you don't know for sure if there's been a breach."

"I've spent a couple of weeks trying to find that out, and I still can't be sure one way or the other. From what I can tell, her abuser has been staying in his own world, but I have heard through the grapevine that he's heading to Vegas today for some big nightclub grand opening."

Dakota pinched the bridge of his nose. Chad and

his father were headed to that event. Or at least they were bragging around town that they were invited. Dakota pulled his laptop closer and sent a message to Trish asking her to find the guest list for the event. If Chad or his father were actually invited, then that would be a cause for concern. Otherwise, merely a coincidence.

Something Dakota didn't believe in.

"What else can you tell me?" Dakota asked.

"I don't really know anything else, but I will give you a piece of advice. Just remember that a man like that isn't going to send someone else to do his dirty work. He's going to want to deal with her himself. You know the enemy; now just watch for him."

"You make it sound like you know he's coming."

"I wish I could say I believed she'd be safe forever, but if I thought that, I wouldn't have sent her to your backyard, now would I?"

"I suppose not." Dakota saw Hank enter the building. "Thanks for the help."

"Anytime, man. Watch your back and take care of that lovely lady and her kid. She's good people."

"You know I will." He set the phone on the desk. "Hey, Hank. Thanks for meeting me."

"Anytime," Hank said. "Do you really think I'm on the need to know right now list?"

Dakota nodded. "Especially now that I've actually spoken with Chauncey."

Hank snagged a chair and pulled it close to the

desk. "I have a feeling I'm going to need to be sitting down for this one."

"Alabama is really Amanda Brolin. She's Josh Brolin's wife."

"Holy fuck," Hank said with his jaw slacked open. "Of all the people I thought it could be, she was not one of them. To be honest, I figured Josh killed his wife and kid. I know there a lot of people who believe that theory."

"Yeah, well, she's alive and well and living in my house."

Hank let out a long breath. "She's a wanted felon."

"Alleged felon." Dakota felt the need to correct that statement. "Chauncey doesn't know for sure if her identity has been compromised, but he did inform me that Josh is headed to Vegas today."

"The grand opening of his cousin's nightclub, who happens to be married to someone who is somehow related to the Hookers," Hank said as he ran a hand over his face. "That's too close to home for me."

"Do we have anyone in Vegas?"

"Boomer is there picking up a witness. I can have him do a quick visual until I can get someone on Josh, but putting a tail on him, as good as we are, is dangerous."

"Not putting one on him is worse," Dakota said. "I need to know my family is safe."

"Family? Are we including Alabama and her son in that statement?"

His heart filled with sensations he didn't want to accept, but he didn't want to ignore them either. "She's my nanny. I moved her into my home. My girls have fallen in love with her and Wyoming, and he's fallen for them. I've fallen for him. Hell, the damn kid calls me Daka and Dada half the time. Yeah. I consider her family."

"Why is it that most of my best men fall in love with the women they end up being charged to protect?" Hank leaned forward, resting his hands on the desk. "Unless Josh does something to get himself arrested, you realize you're aiding and abetting?"

"Is that going to be a problem?"

Hank shook his head. "But I want you to think about the fact that like her, you are now going to be looking over your shoulder unless someone takes that man down."

"I'm up for the task, how about you?"

Hank laughed. "It's not going to happen overnight, but let's start a think tank first thing Monday morning. In the meantime, I'll make sure someone's got eyes on Josh. Now, go home and enjoy Valentine's Day with *your family*."

"Thanks." Dakota closed his laptop. His pulse picked up, and the corners of his mouth tugged into a smile.

He had an epic family dinner planned with a romantic nightcap for after the kids went to bed. It was going to be perfect.

ALABAMA STRETCHED out on the sofa in the main family room. The fire crackled in the background. Sky, River, and Wyoming sat on the floor with blocks and puzzles while one of their favorite Disney movies played in the background.

Buster jumped from the floor and started barking like a madman. He raced to the front door, Apollo running after him, yelping all the way.

Alabama jerked upright and glanced out the window. Ugh.

"What is *she* doing here?" River asked with a roll of her eyes.

"Bringing Daddy a Valentine's Day gift, no doubt," Sky said with big adult dose of sarcasm. "Can we tell her you're dating Daddy and to go away?"

Alabama stifled a laugh. "No. That would be rude."

"But she won't leave him alone, and he's too nice to be mean about it," Sky said. The little girl was way too mature for her age and wise beyond her years.

"You three stay here. I'll handle Teresa." While her knees no longer knocked together as she approached the front door, her nerves were still a little frayed. Handling passive aggressive women was never her strong suit, but with her newfound confidence, she might be able to handle Teresa. Alabama twisted the door handle and pulled it back with a big smile. "Hello, Teresa. What brings you by today?"

Teresa frowned. "What are you doing in Dakota's house on the weekend?"

Oh. This was going to be fun. "I live here."

"You what?" Teresa stood there with her mouth wide open, holding a basket of goodies.

"I live in the in-law apartment." Alabama decided to be honest. There was no point in pushing Teresa's buttons.

"Where's Dakota?"

"He had to go into the office today."

She glanced at the watch on her wrist. "It's getting late. I bet he'll be home soon. I'll just wait."

Buster continued to bark, but Alabama did her best to ignore the beast.

"I don't think that's a good idea. We have plans as soon as he returns. But I'm happy to tell him you stopped by."

"Plans? To do what?" Teresa asked.

Alabama shrugged. "He won't tell me. Some big Valentine's Day surprise."

Teresa narrowed her eyes and pursed her lips. "Like a date?"

"Exactly like a date." Alabama glanced down at the basket in Teresa's hands. "Is that for Dakota and the girls? I can take that and give it to them if you want, but in the future, I'd appreciate it if you didn't bring my boyfriend gifts."

"You really shouldn't tell lies like that. Dakota won't like it," Teresa said.

A fancy vehicle slowed by the entrance to the ranch.

Her heart skipped a beat when the shiny limo pulled into the driveway. Her muscles froze in place. No one in these parts drove around in a car like that. The only person she knew who would use that mode of transportation should be two thousand miles away.

"As a matter of fact, I'm going to text him right now and tell him what you're saying," Teresa continued.

"You go right ahead." Alabama's vocal cords barely worked.

Teresa glanced over her shoulder. "Who's that?"

"I think you should go now, but don't forget to send that text to Dakota. And while you're at it, tell him we have unexpected company." God, she hoped Teresa was as nosy as she thought she was and that she would be texting Dakota before she was even out of the driveway.

"I won't do your bidding," Teresa said in a huff. She dropped the basket and turned on her heels. "But I am going to warn Dakota. You're worse than his last nanny." Teresa stomped through the snow and climbed into her SUV. The engine revved, and she peeled out of the driveway.

The driver stepped from the front of the limo and opened the back door.

"Girls. Take my phone and Wyoming, go into the apartment, and lock yourselves in my bedroom. Call your father. Tell him Josh is here. Do it now."

"Is everything okay?" Sky asked.

Alabama turned. "Just do it. No questions. Don't come out unless I tell you to or your father does, got it?"

Sky nodded as she scooped up Wyoming into her arms.

River raced past her sister. "What's going on? Who's out there?"

Alabama took River by the forearms. "He's a bad man, and he's come here to hurt me and Wyoming. Please. Just do as I ask. Okay?"

River nodded, and then both girls went running with Wyoming down the hallway.

Alabama took a deep breath and turned. Gasping, she covered her mouth.

Josh stood at the bottom of the steps. "Honey, I'm home."

"Hold up."

Dakota paused by the front door and glanced over his shoulder. "What's up, Hank?"

"I just heard from Boomer. Josh never made it to

Vegas. He switched planes in Chicago and booked a private charter."

"To where?" he asked as his phone buzzed five times in his back pocket. He pulled it out and glanced at the screen.

Two messages from Teresa.

And three from Alabama.

That couldn't be good, but he didn't feel like dealing with that kind of drama just yet.

"Here. He landed forty-five minutes ago," Hank said.

"You've got to be fucking kidding me?" Dakota dropped everything in his hands to the ground except his phone. Frantically, he tapped at the screen.

Teresa: Your nanny is telling everyone you're dating.

Teresa: And some fancy rich guy is here visiting her.

Fuck.

Alabama: Daddy, it's Sky. Alabama told us to lock ourselves in her bedroom.

Alabama: She said to tell you Josh is here.

Alabama: She said he's a bad man. Daddy, hurry!

"Josh is at my house," Dakota said. He pushed aside the emotional fury that swirled in his gut and let his training and experience guide his brain. If he was going to save his family, he had to think and act like the professional he was.

"I'll drive. The back roads have been plowed, so we're only ten minutes away. You call Clayton and Viper."

Dakota tossed his boss his truck keys. "If he touches my girls or Wyoming, I won't be held responsible for killing him."

"What about Alabama?"

"She's one of my girls."

"I hear you loud and clear," Hank said as he climbed into the pickup. "But let's not go in half-cocked. We have ten minutes to figure out a plan."

"That's simple. Sky, River, and Wyoming are locked in the apartment bedroom. That's the back of the house, and we can have Viper or Clayton get them going totally unnoticed while I deal with Josh and you get Alabama to safety."

"While I would want to strangle the bastard myself too, we need to call the locals. We need to nail this bastard with proof so Alabama can live her life without fear."

Dakota placed both hands on the dashboard. "If that doesn't work, we go back to me killing him."

CHAPTER 10

ALABAMA STUMBLED backward into the family room. Apollo jumped on her, wagging his tail, but Buster didn't take too kindly to the man sauntering through the door.

"Shut that fucking dog up," Josh said.

"Buster, quiet," she commanded.

Buster whined.

"How about the stupid animals go outside where they belong." Josh actually kicked both dogs out the door before slamming it shut. "Did you actually think I wouldn't find you?"

"Why do you even care? You don't love me, and I don't love you."

He stood over her with his hands on his hips, shaking his head. "Of course I love you. I've spent a small fortune looking for you; that's how much I love you." He lifted his foot, drawing it back. "It pains me so that you always make me do things like this."

She stiffened her body, preparing for the blow.

And Josh didn't disappoint.

She groaned as the toe of his very expensive Italian shoes landed directly on her hip bone. "I'm not making you do anything." She pushed herself toward the far wall and forced herself to her feet. "What do you want?"

"For starters, I want you and our son to come home," he said, taking a few small steps in her direction.

She could hear Buster scratching and whining at the front door. It would be music to her ears if she heard him barking. That would mean something or someone was lurking around outside. She continued to move across the back wall in the direction of the kitchen. There were knives and other weapons there. But that would also bring Josh closer to the kids.

Maybe she needed to rethink that plan.

"I'm not going anywhere with you, and neither is *my* son."

Josh laughed. "That's what you think." He ran a finger across the mantel above the fireplace and lifted the picture of Dakota with his family. "Who are these people?"

"I work for them," she said.

"Where are they?"

"Out. But they will be home any minute, and you don't want to mess with him. He's ex-military."

"I don't give a fuck what he used to be. Now I saw our little boy in here with two girls. Where'd you send them? Where are they hiding?"

"They aren't here."

Josh lunged forward.

She tried to turn and run, but he grabbed her by the hair. "You know I can't stand it when you lie to me." He tugged hard, spinning her around until his knuckles smashed into her left cheekbone. She dropped to the floor, landing on her knees, but jerked back up as he lifted her to her feet by her hair.

Her scalp burned and stung as wads of hair were pulled out. Heat flashed in her face, and a sharp pain pulsed behind her eye.

"I'll keep using you as a punching bag until you tell me."

"Have at it," she said. There was no way she was letting him anywhere near the kids. She dug her heels into the area rug and twisted her body, swinging her right arm until her own fist connected with his chin.

He jerked back a few inches and then laughed. "Keep that up, sweetheart. I need a few bruises so that when I go to the press, I'll have a good story to tell about how volatile you are and how your mental illness got the better of you."

"Yeah. And how will you explain the beating

you're giving me?" She curled her fingers around his wrist, hoping to ease the pressure on her head.

"I won't have to. Once I have my son, you're going to kill yourself. Of course, there will be a note, explaining your insanity—"

"You're the fucking crazy one. I'm never letting you take Wyoming. Ever." She fisted both hands and started pounding at his chest as hard as she could.

"Bitch," he muttered, tossing her into the hutch. Plates and glasses fell to the ground, shattering around her body. She stepped on a piece of glass as she tried to run down the hallway. She crumpled to the floor.

"Where are they? Tell me now, and I won't hurt those two little girls. But keep making me beat it out of you, and I'll have to do the same to them."

"Over my dead body." The taste of metal dribbled down her throat. She rolled to all fours.

His foot connected to her gut.

She held her breath and continued to try to stand.

But he kicked her again.

And again.

Lying flat on the floor, she slithered like a snake toward the kitchen.

Josh grabbed her by the ankle and yanked. He rolled her to the side. He stood over her, smiling like the devil. "Why on earth would you name *my* son Wyoming. That's a horrible name for a Brolin." He grabbed her by the shirt and cocked his fist. It landed on her right cheek.

Her head slammed back onto the floor. It felt as though someone put an ice pick through her brain. She blinked through the pain, trying to gain focus. Through the ringing in her ears, she could hear Buster barking like crazy.

That gave her hope until he abruptly stopped.

Josh stepped over her and headed toward the apartment door. "I'll just check every room in this hellhole until I find them."

She leaped to her feet and threw herself at Josh, smacking his nose with the palm of her hand.

"Fucking bitch." He grabbed her by the neck and slammed her into the wall, lifting her feet off the ground.

She held on to his wrists as her legs dangled. She gasped for air.

"Get your goddamned hands off her," Dakota's voice bounced around in her mind.

A second later, Clayton had Josh pushed down on the ground while he was slapping handcuffs on him, and Dakota lifted her into his arms and carried her over to the sofa.

"Wyoming. And the girls? Where are they?" she cried out.

"They are fine," Dakota said. "Hank got them from the bedroom window. He's going to take them away for a bit until we get Josh out of here and you loaded up in an ambulance."

She tried to sit up, but her sides felt like something snapped. Her vision blurred, and it hurt like hell to take a deep breath. "The kids. They're okay?"

Dakota nodded. "You, on the other hand, don't look so good."

"You should see the other guy."

Dakota laughed. "I'm pretty sure you broke his nose."

"Good." Carefully, she leaned back on the sofa and closed her eyes. "I tried to protect the kids."

"You didn't try. You succeeded," Dakota whispered right before he pressed his lips against her neck. "If I didn't know better, I'd think you were after my job."

She waved a hand in the air. "No. But Teresa is after my boyfriend."

"You don't have to worry about that. Your boyfriend has been struck by cupid, and he only has eyes for you."

"That's nice," she mumbled. "My head hurts." She let the darkness engulf her while wondering if Dakota had actually said those words or if she dreamed them.

DAKOTA PACED in the waiting room. He knew she'd

taken a good beating, but the fact she needed surgery for some internal bleeding made him see red. Thank God they'd removed Josh, because if he'd been anywhere near Dakota, he would be sitting in a cell right now, and that wouldn't have been good.

"Relax, man. She's fine. They said the surgery went well, and once she's in recovery, they will come get you." Clayton sat in the corner of the waiting room with his legs crossed and a book in his hands as if he didn't have a care in the world.

"Easy for you to say. She didn't have to go under the knife because of you."

"Right, because you're the one who kicked her with a steel toe designer shoe in the gut," Clayton said with a heavy dose of sarcasm. "And don't start in on the whole idea that if you had acted sooner, this wouldn't have happened. We had no way of knowing that Hooker had figured out who she was and sold that information to Josh."

Dakota plopped himself down on one of the hard metal chairs. "But we knew the connection. We should have seen it coming and tried to prevent it."

"How? How do you suppose we were going to do that without potentially giving up Alabama's identity and whereabouts? You did everything right. And that lady of yours, she's one feisty woman. She managed to keep him from the kids for a good half hour before we could get to her."

"Don't remind me." Dakota pinched the bridge of

his nose and exhaled all the air in his lungs in one big swish. "It broke my heart to see her like that."

"I know it did." Clayton slapped him on the shoulder. "But you have to remember she chose to stay and fight him. She did that because she wants a life, and I'm going to take a wild guess that she wants a life with you and your daughters."

"I'm hoping that's the case," Dakota admitted.

"Here comes the doctor." Clayton pointed down the hallway.

Dakota was on his feet and standing in front of the doctor in seconds flat. "How is Alabama doing? Is she in the recovery room now? Can I see her?"

"She's doing great. She's back in her room. Like I said, since it's so late, we'll keep her overnight, but she'll be ready to go home in the morning." The doctor put her hands in her lab coat pockets. "She does have a lot of swelling around her eye, and I suggested she see a specialist since her vision is still pretty blurry, but otherwise, she's just fine."

"Thanks, Doc. I really appreciate it."

"Anytime." The doctor nodded and then disappeared back down the hallway.

"I'm going to head home," Clayton said. "Shall I tell the girls you're staying here tonight?"

"Yeah. I'll come by first thing in the morning and get them and Wyoming when I bring Alabama home." Dakota outstretched his arm. "Thanks for everything."

With a thick lump in his throat and his heart beating out of his chest, he made his way toward Alabama's private room. Just in case, while everything got sorted out, they placed an arm guard at her door. It was overkill, but he appreciated the effort.

He stepped into the room, and his lungs deflated as he stared at her black and blue swollen face.

She shifted in her bed, adjusting the bed covers.

"Let me help you with that." He strolled to her side and fluffed her pillow before bending over and kissing her forehead, careful not to touch any of her bruises. "The doctor says everything went well with the surgery."

"Where's Wyoming?" she asked.

"With Sage." He sat on the edge of the bed and took her hand. "Josh isn't just being arrested for what he did today. Candice has given the Feds some information that will not only take down the Hookers, but will put Josh and his father away for many years. It's a done deal. Trust me on this."

She covered her mouth and gasped. "Are you sure? Leslie thought it was all in the bag."

"The FBI had an undercover agent working inside Josh's organization. That person helped your nurse get you out, and during this last year, he gathered enough information to put that asshole away for good. I'm just sorry it didn't happen before he did this." He reached out and gently ran his index finger across her cheek. "I'm so sorry I didn't get there sooner."

"I'm just glad he didn't hurt the kids."

"You made sure of that," he said. "You protected my girls. Thank you."

She laughed, clutching her stomach. "I brought trouble to your doorstep."

"The only thing you brought to my house was love." He jerked his head back. "Why did you pick the last name Love? It's an unusual name for someone on the run."

"Where's my necklace?" she asked.

He dug through her belongings until he found it.

"Open it. Behind the picture of me and Wyoming is a picture of me and my parents when I was a kid."

"You're not supposed to keep anything from your past." He clicked open the clasp and pulled out the small picture. In the background of the image was a sign that read: *Alabama Love, best biscuits and grits in town.*

"When I was a little girl, my parents used to take me to Maryland to visit my grandparents. They lived in this cute little town and their favorite restaurant was Alabama Love. We stopped going when I was like ten, and I had honestly forgotten about it for years until about a month before I left Josh."

"You forgot?" he asked with an arched brow.

"I just didn't think about it, and thankfully, I never talked to Josh about it. I was going through some things I had taken from my parents' house that were in storage because Josh wanted me to toss it all, and I came across that picture. It reminded me of what life should be like for a kid. When I got the chance to leave, that name just seemed perfect."

"It is perfect," he said, lifting her hand to his lips. "You're perfect and wonderful, and I have a confession to make that might make you want to run away."

"Oh yeah, what's that?" she asked.

"I'm falling madly in love with you."

A single tear rolled down her cheek. "You really are Mr. Wonderful."

"Does that mean the feeling is mutual?"

She smiled. "You might need to ask me that again when I'm not all doped up on medication, but yes. I'm falling head over heels in love with you."

EPILOGUE

Six months later...

Alabama flicked the oven light off and checked the time. Ten minutes. Her heart fluttered. "This meal better come out right," she mumbled. She'd gotten a lot better at cooking, but this was one of Dakota's favorites, and she wanted to do it right.

Or at least good enough that he didn't toss it down the garbage disposal and order a pizza.

Both Buster and Apollo started barking and running in circles the second Dakota's headlights cut through the dark night.

"Daddy's home," River exclaimed as she skipped through the kitchen wearing cowboy boots and a tutu.

"Da Da." Wyoming followed a few steps behind,

bumping into the walls and falling twice. They'd stopped correcting him from calling Dakota dad, but neither one of them had ever addressed the topic. Of course, she still slept in the apartment and he upstairs. Well, they each pretended to wake up in their own rooms, making sure they snuck out before the girls woke.

Only, Sky saw Alabama sneaking out of Dakota's room this morning.

Which was why Alabama needed to have a deep conversation with Dakota about the way things were so they could answer the kids questions the same way, especially with the big news she had to share.

Butterflies filled her stomach. The first few months after Josh had shown up had been difficult. A lot of her old fears resurfaced, and of course, the Feds needed her statement. After that, she and Dakota were taking their time getting to know one another. Loving each other wasn't a question. Their love came easy and naturally. But they both had baggage and children and a past. She also wanted to make sure she was never disrespecting River and Sky's mother. Lunar always needed to be a part of their lives.

Even if they started a family of their own.

Another thing they mentioned in passing, but it was going to be a discussion for a later date.

Well, that later date was today.

Sky came barreling down the stairs. "Did I hear Dad pull in?"

"You sure did." Dakota strolled into the kitchen with Wyoming on his back and River doing a dance between his legs. "How was school?"

"I hate the fifth grade," Sky said, slumping down at the kitchen table. "And I hate math."

"I suck at it, or I would have helped her." Alabama leaned in and stole a brief kiss, but Dakota had other plans as he pulled her closer and turned up the heat.

Wyoming covered his eyes and made a funny noise, mimicking River.

"Get a room," Sky said. "Oh, wait. You have two; you just can't pick one."

"Excuse me?" Dakota said.

The oven dinged.

"You, young lady, are saved by the bell. Everyone go clean up for dinner." Dakota set Wyoming on the floor. "Sky, take him and help him."

"Daddy, do I have to?"

"Sky. Remember what we talked about earlier today?"

"Oh. Yeah. Okay."

Alabama pulled the shepherd's pie out of the oven. It smelled good. But that didn't mean it tasted good. "I told you she saw me this morning."

"I know." Dakota leaned against the counter. "I had a chat with her on the way to school this morning. She knows way too much about sex and stuff."

"She made me blush, but I want us to be on the

same page when we answer these questions, because River is starting with the questions."

He ran a hand over his scruffy face. "I know. She's been sending me interesting text messages for days now. I'm not sure what to do."

"What do you mean?"

"Well, she's been sending pictures of these and asking me when I'm going to get you one." He dug into his pocket and pulled out a small black velvet box.

"Oh, my God." Her eyes stung. She clutched the pendant dangling from her neck.

He flipped open the top and inside rested a silver ring with a diamond in the middle. It wasn't huge or flashy, but it wasn't tiny either. "I love you. We're already a family, but I want to make it official." He dug into his pocket. "And I want to officially adopt Wyoming, if you'll let me."

She covered her mouth and swallowed a guttural sob. She glanced between the ring and him.

"Will you marry me?"

"Before I answer that, I need to tell you something," she managed to croak out. "You might want to sit down for this."

"Oh, I don't like the way this is going," he said. "And I'm good standing."

"Okay." She cleared her throat. No reason to beat around the bush. Might as well just say it. "I'm pregnant."

He dropped the ring. It bounced on the floor.

Sky, River, and Wyoming all came racing into the kitchen.

"A baby!" Sky screamed.

"I'm going to be a big sister?" River asked. "Wyoming is going to be a big brother?"

"I think Daddy needs to sit down," Dakota said as he made his way to the kitchen table. He pulled back the chair and slowly lowered himself. "I didn't see that coming."

"Me neither," she admitted. "I haven't been to the doctor, but I took the test this morning."

"Those things are pretty accurate."

"That they are," she said.

"Alabama," River said, holding out the ring. "You didn't answer Daddy. Are you going to marry him and be our mom?"

Oh, that statement knocked her to her knees. She knelt in front of River. "I can never take the place of your mama. She's always going to be a big part of your life, and I want that."

"But you're going to marry Daddy, right?" Sky asked.

"Yeah. I'd like to know the answer to that question." Dakota pulled her to his lap. He took the ring and slipped it on her finger. "So, are we going to make this official?"

"Yes. I love you." She cupped his face and planted a wet kiss on his lips.

"Wonderful," Sky said. "Now they don't have to sneak around anymore, and they can just sleep in the same bed."

"I'm not ready for her to be a teenager," Dakota whispered.

"Get ready for it times four."

Special Forces Operation Alpha

BURNING DESIRE

BURNING KISS

BURNING SKIES

BURNING LIES

BURNING HEART

BURNING BED

REMEMBER ME ALWAYS

The Brotherhood Protectors

ROUGH JUSTICE

ROUGH AROUND THE EDGES

ROUGH RIDE

ROUGH EDGE

ROUGH BEAUTY

A Family Affair

Nightshade

A Christmas Getaway

Taking A Risk

Tee Time

The Twilight Crossing Series

THE BLIND DATE

SPRING FLING

SUMMER'S GONE

WINTER WEDDING

Witches and Werewolves

LADY SASS

ALL THAT SASS

Coming soon!

NEON SASS

PAINTING SASS

Boxsets

LOVE CHRISTMAS, MOVIES

UNFORGETABLE PASSION

UNFORGETABLE CHARMERS

A NIGHT SHE'LL REMEMBER

SWEET AND SASSY IN THE SNOW

SWEET AND SASSY PRINCE CHARMING

PROTECT AND DESIRE

SWEET AND SASSY BABY LOVE

CHRISTMAS AT MISTLETOE LODGE

THE PLAYERS: OVERCOMING THE ODDS

CHRISTMAS SHORTS

CHRISTMAS DREAMS

All That Glitters

INVINCIBLE SECRETS

UNFORGETABLE SUSPENSE

Nove*llas*

NIGHTSHADE

A CHRISTMAS GETAWAY

TAKING A RISK

WHISPERS

Welcome to my World! I'm a USA Today Bestseller of Romantic Suspense, Contemporary Romance, and Paranormal Romance.

I first started writing while carting my kids to one hockey rink after the other, averaging 170 games per year between 3 kids in 2 countries and 5 states. My first book, IN TWO WEEKS was originally published in 2007. In 2010 I helped form a publishing company (Cool Gus Publishing) with NY Times Bestselling Author Bob Mayer where I ran the technical side of the business through 2016.

I'm currently enjoying the next phase of my life...the empty NESTER! My husband and I spend our winters in Jupiter, Florida and our summers in Rochester, NY. We have three amazing children who have all gone off to carve out their places in the world, while I continue to craft stories that I hope will make you readers feel good and put a smile on your face.

Sign up for my Newsletter
(https://dl.bookfunnel.com/6atcf7g1be)

where I often give away free books before publication.

*Join my private Facebook group
(https://www.facebook.com/groups/191706547909047/)
where she posts exclusive excerpts and discuss all things
murder and love!*

Never miss a new release. Follow me on

Amazon:amazon.com/author/jentalty

And on

Bookbub: bookbub.com/authors/jen-talty

BROTHERHOOD PROTECTORS

ORIGINAL SERIES BY ELLE JAMES

Brotherhood Protectors Series

Montana SEAL (#1)

Bride Protector SEAL (#2)

Montana D-Force (#3)

Cowboy D-Force (#4)

Montana Ranger (#5)

Montana Dog Soldier (#6)

Montana SEAL Daddy (#7)

Montana Ranger's Wedding Vow (#8)

Montana SEAL Undercover Daddy (#9)

Cape Cod SEAL Rescue (#10)

Montana SEAL Friendly Fire (#11)

Montana SEAL's Mail-Order Bride (#12)

SEAL Justice (#13)

Ranger Creed (#14)

Delta Force Strong (#15)

Montana Rescue (Sleeper SEAL)

Hot SEAL Salty Dog (SEALs in Paradise)

Hot SEAL Hawaiian Nights (SEALs in Paradise)

ABOUT ELLE JAMES

ELLE JAMES also writing as MYLA JACKSON is a *New York Times* and *USA Today* Bestselling author of books including cowboys, intrigues and paranormal adventures that keep her readers on the edges of their seats. With over eighty works in a variety of sub-genres and lengths she has published with Harlequin, Samhain, Ellora's Cave, Kensington, Cleis Press, and Avon. When she's not at her computer, she's traveling, snow skiing, boating, or riding her ATV, dreaming up new stories. Learn more about Elle James at www.ellejames.com

Website | Facebook | Twitter | GoodReads | Newsletter | BookBub | Amazon

Follow Elle!
www.ellejames.com
ellejames@ellejames.com

facebook.com/ellejamesauthor
twitter.com/ElleJamesAuthor